A baby she'd never carried inside her...

Never held in her arms. Never even seen. And yet he was already there in her heart. A son. Rachel slowly let that sink in.

She had a child, and Esterman's people might hurt him before they could find him.

"I'd given up hope of ever having a baby," she admitted. She ran her fingers over the child's picture. "Especially when you refused to let me use the embryos after we separated."

"Yes."

That was it. The sum total of Jared's response. But Rachel didn't hold it against him. She wasn't sure how she was supposed to respond, either. Most couples had nine months to build up to a moment like this. Nine months of hope, planning and dreams. Their dream was one big nightmare.

"We have to find him...."

Dear Harlequin Intrigue Reader,

We wind up a great summer with a *bang* this month! Linda O. Johnston continues the hugely popular COLORADO CONFIDENTIAL series with *Special Agent Nanny*. Don't forget to look for the Harlequin special-release anthology next month featuring *USA TODAY* bestselling author Jasmine Cresswell, our very own Amanda Stevens and Harlequin Historicals author Debra Lee Brown. And not to worry, the series continues with two more Harlequin Intrigue titles in November and December.

Joyce Sullivan concludes her companion series THE COLLINGWOOD HEIRS with *Operation Bassinet*. Find out how this family solves a fiendish plot and finds happiness in one fell swoop. Rounding out the month are two exciting stories. Rising star Delores Fossen takes a unique perspective on the classic secret-baby plot in *Confiscated Conception*, and a very sexy *Cowboy PI* is determined to get to the bottom of one woman's mystery in an all-Western story by Jean Barrett.

Finally, in case you haven't heard, next month Harlequin Intrigue is increasing its publishing schedule to include two more fantastic romantic suspense books. That's *six* titles per month! More variety, more of your favorite authors and of course, more excitement.

It's a thrilling time for us, and we want to thank all of our loyal readers for remaining true to Harlequin Intrigue. And if you are just learning about our brand of breathtaking romantic suspense, fasten your seat belts for an edge-of-your-seat reading experience. Welcome aboard!

Sincerely,

Denise O'Sullivan
Senior Editor, Harlequin Intrigue

CONFISCATED CONCEPTION

DELORES FOSSEN

TORONTO • NEW YORK • LONDON
AMSTERDAM • PARIS • SYDNEY • HAMBURG
STOCKHOLM • ATHENS • TOKYO • MILAN • MADRID
PRAGUE • WARSAW • BUDAPEST • AUCKLAND

ISBN 0-373-22727-2

CONFISCATED CONCEPTION

ABOUT THE AUTHOR

Imagine a family tree that includes Texas cowboys, Choctaw and Cherokee Indians, a Louisiana pirate and a Scottish rebel who battled side by side with William Wallace. With ancestors like that, it's easy to understand why Texas author and former air force captain Delores Fossen feels as if she was genetically predisposed to writing romances. Along the way to fulfilling her DNA destiny, Delores married an air force Top Gun who just happens to be of Viking descent. With all those romantic bases covered, she doesn't have to look too far for inspiration.

Books by Delores Fossen

HARLEQUIN INTRIGUE
648—HIS CHILD
679—A MAN WORTH REMEMBERING
704—MARCHING ORDERS
727—CONFISCATED CONCEPTION

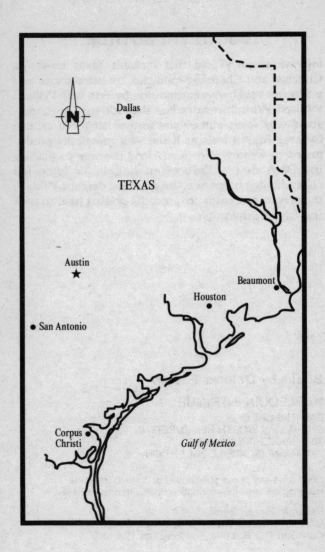

CAST OF CHARACTERS

Lieutenant Jared Dillard—Even though he still cares for his soon-to-be ex-wife, Rachel, he believes she's out of his life for good—until he receives word that someone stole the fertilized embryo they stored years ago. Now there's a child—their child—and the baby will die if Jared and Rachel don't work together to find him.

Rachel Dillard—She's been in protective custody for over a year, and just hours before she's supposed to testify against her dirty dealing boss, she learns that she has a newborn son. If she doesn't testify, a killer will go free, but if she takes the stand, her child will die.

Clarence Esterman—Rachel's former boss would do anything to stop her from testifying against him.

Sergeant Colby Meredith—Is he a cop on the take with orders from Esterman to assassinate Jared?

Lyle Brewer—Clarence Esterman's lawyer. He's possibly Esterman's silent partner and the one who has Rachel and Jared's baby.

Donald Livingston—Is this prison warden the mastermind behind Esterman's plan to stop Rachel from testifying, or is he simply a pawn in a dangerous game?

To my brother, Mike, and his wife, Ann Marie

Chapter One

Jared heard the footsteps a split second before the man aimed a semiautomatic at his head.

"Don't move," the officer ordered. He stepped around the side of the ranch house and approached Jared as if he were a cobra ready to strike. In a way, he was.

With the thick envelope still clutched in his hand, Jared lifted his arms in a show of surrender. "I'm Lieutenant Dillard, San Antonio PD. I believe you're expecting me?"

"It's all right, Smitty," a woman called out from inside the house. "He's Rachel's husband. I recognize him." The door opened, and Detective Miller, the dark-haired officer on the other side, motioned for Jared to enter.

"Lieutenant Dillard," she greeted. "I wish you were here under different circumstances."

The officer glanced at the envelope, and from the

somber expression on her thin face it was clear that she thought it contained the divorce papers that Jared had mentioned on the phone.

It didn't.

But it would have been far better if it had.

Jared stepped inside and made a mental note of the weapons that were neatly arranged in a rack next to the door. Side arms and rifles for backup. Extra magazines of ammunition. Ditto for the two Texas Rangers posted at the checkpoint at the end of the road. They were armed to the hilt.

Maybe the four peace officers wouldn't try to use those weapons against him before this visit was over.

He glanced around the sparsely furnished place and spotted Rachel right away. She was in the adjoining room that had been converted to a gym of sorts. She was barefoot. Her shoulder-length dark blond hair was pulled into a sleek ponytail. She wore a pair of loose gray boxers and a red sleeveless T-shirt.

Oh, man.

She looked good. It'd been months since Jared had last seen her and well over a year since he'd had her in his bed. But even after all that time and after everything that had gone on between them, the thought of making love to Rachel still set his blood on fire.

He had too-vivid memories of her naked body slick with perspiration. The feel of her firm breasts beneath his hands. The scent of her arousal mixed with his. The heat of her mouth. The eagerness of her touch.

Which obviously wouldn't be so eager now.

Jared watched as she pounded her fists and then her forearms into the punching bag. The blows weren't random but part of a workout routine. Shaolin boxing. And from the looks of things, she wasn't a beginner.

"Hello, Jared. You're early. I didn't expect you for another hour." Rachel spared him a cool glance with those intense jungle-green eyes before she peeled off her scarred boxing gloves. She picked up a bottle of water from a weight bench, took her time drinking it and then strolled to the window.

Ah, the ice princess act. Her favorite. He recognized it immediately. It probably fooled her bodyguards, but it sure as hell didn't fool him. She was riled by his visit.

Interesting.

"When did you take up Shaolin boxing?" he asked, walking toward her.

Rachel wiped the perspiration from her forehead with the back of her hand. "About a year ago."

Of course. It made sense. After all, there was a reason she was in protective custody. This was probably her way of dealing with the constant fear and stress from Clarence Esterman's death threats.

"You're good at it."

She shrugged. "Well, if I'm ever accosted by a punching bag in a dark alley, I'll be able to hold my own." The comment might have been lighthearted, but that lightheartedness didn't quite make it to her voice. She flexed her eyebrows, a mild indication that the chitchat was over. "Let me get a pen so I can sign those papers."

So much for breaking the ice. This obviously wasn't an ice-breaking sort of moment. Unfortunately, he had to proceed anyway.

Jared went to her, slipped his arm around her waist. Before she could protest their bodily contact— or use one of those Shaolin boxing moves on him— he upped the ante. He crushed his mouth to hers.

The kiss was, well, *interesting*, too. Even though it was supposed to be all for show, it sent a jolt of pure heat through him. Too bad he couldn't say the same for Rachel. If she felt any heat, it was likely from temper and not passion. She shoved her forearm against his abs and jerked away. Jared didn't let her get too far.

"Play along," he whispered against her ear. He slipped the thick envelope into the inside pocket of his jacket. "It's important."

No cool dismissive glance from her this time. Rachel's scalpel-sharp gaze sliced him, her eyes asking a lot of tough questions. Questions he couldn't begin to answer in front of the other officers.

Jared touched her arm with his fingers and rubbed softly. More of the pretense. It was a gesture meant to comfort and reassure.

It didn't work.

He felt her muscles tighten even more.

"Could you give us some time alone?" Jared asked the detectives. He didn't look back at Miller and Smith, nor did he take his attention off the obviously irritated woman in front of him. "Rachel's going in the Witness Protection Program after she testifies against Clarence Esterman this afternoon, so this is my last chance to be with her."

Detective Miller practically marched across the room and joined them. "Sorry, but I'm not allowed to let Rachel out of my sight. Especially not today."

Jared gave her his best wise-guy glare. "Then, you'd better brace yourself for one helluva peep show, Detective, because I intend to take my *wife* in the bedroom and do my best to *talk* her out of this divorce."

Rachel opened her mouth and then closed it just as quickly. She pulled her eyebrows together. Jared gave her arm a gentle squeeze, hoping it would buy him a little more cooperation. It bought him a scowl.

"I have orders from the captain—"

"I'm a cop," Jared reminded Miller. "Head of

Special Investigations and your superior officer. The captain's order is that Rachel be guarded at all times. She will be—by me—and it'll happen in the bedroom.''

Jared didn't wait to see if Rachel or Miller would call his bluff. He latched onto Rachel and got her moving toward the back of the house.

''What's this all about?'' Rachel demanded in an angry whisper.

Jared didn't answer. Not with the detectives right behind them in the hallway. He'd studied the floor plan of the house so he knew where her living quarters were. He maneuvered Rachel into the makeshift suite and slammed the door before Miller could invite herself in.

''I don't have time to explain everything,'' Jared informed her. ''I have to get you out of here—*now.*''

Surprise and then outrage raced through her eyes. It was an understandable reaction. He was feeling plenty of outrage himself.

Jared clamped his hand over her mouth before she could voice her emotions. ''Just listen.''

But she didn't. Rachel shoved his hand away. ''I don't know what kind of game you're playing, but I want no part of it, understand? Just give me the divorce papers, damn it, and I'll sign them.''

''There are no divorce papers.''

Other than a somewhat shocked look, Rachel didn't have time to react to that news flash.

"Rachel?" Detective Miller called out. "Are you sure you're all right in there?"

Jared moved quickly when he heard the door open, and he cursed himself for not locking it. It was time to beef up the charade, since Miller obviously wasn't backing off.

He snapped Rachel to him and kissed her as if they hadn't been separated for the past fourteen months. In the same motion, he slid his hand beneath her T-shirt. With everything else going on, he sure as hell shouldn't have noticed that she was wearing only a tiny, silky swatch of a bra.

Lace, at that.

Miller cleared her throat. "If you need me, Rachel, just yell. I'll be right outside."

The moment Miller shut the door, Rachel pushed Jared away from her. "What the heck is wrong with you?"

"Plenty." Jared hurried to the door and locked it. "It's been a really bad night, and the morning hasn't gotten any better."

Not wasting any time, he went to the closet. It was in perfect order. As he'd known it would be. Rachel arranged and organized things when she was nervous. And when she was really nervous, she paced.

He figured she'd be pacing and organizing a lot before this was over.

Jared grabbed a pair of running shoes and jeans from the closet and thrust them into her hands. "I don't have time to soothe your doubts or convince you that I'm doing the right thing. I have to get you out of here."

"I'm not going anywhere with you." Rachel dropped the shoes on the floor, but with incensed tugs and jerks, she did put on the jeans over her workout shorts. "In a little less than three hours, I'm leaving to testify against Clarence Esterman, and the officers outside will be the ones driving me. Not you."

"You can't testify," Jared said. "Not today, anyway."

"Judas Priest!" Rachel propped her hands on her hips and stared at him. "Are you saying there's been another trial delay? Because if there has been—"

She stopped, and just like that, the color drained from her face. She slowly sank onto the edge of the bed. "My God, did Esterman get to you? Did he send you here to try to talk me out of testifying?"

Jared cursed. Hell. She obviously thought he was lower than slime to have suggested something like that. It meant there was nothing he could say that would make her change her mind about leaving with him.

Instead, he'd have to show her.

Jared finished putting on her shoes, tied the laces with far more force than required and then reached inside his jacket. He yanked out the envelope.

"I told you earlier on the phone that I'd sign the divorce papers," she continued, her voice getting more indignant with each word. "There's no reason for us to go through this—whatever the heck *this* is. You can have the town house. The car. Everything. I'll need to start fresh anyway, once they give me a new identity."

Jared ignored her, opened the envelope and extracted the photo of the newborn baby. When she refused to take it, he dropped it on the bed next to her.

Rachel glanced at it and shrugged. "So? What does that have to do with our divorce or with me testifying against my former boss?"

He had to unclench his jaw so he could speak. "I've been told that the baby in that photo is my son."

Her head whipped up, her eyes narrowed and accusing. He could almost see her process that bit of startling information. She didn't process it well. With reason. Before they'd gone their separate ways, Rachel and he had spent two long years trying to conceive a child.

They'd failed.

And so had their marriage.

Rachel swallowed hard. "You have a son?"

Jared wasn't immune to the hurt he saw on her face. But that hurt was nothing compared to what he'd no doubt see when he told her the rest.

"It seems that way. He's six days old." Jared hadn't meant his explanation to grind to a halt, but then, he hadn't counted on his mouth turning to dust either. Hell. He hated the people who'd set all of this in motion.

Rachel shook a head, a nervous shudder. Obviously she didn't understand. But how could she possibly understand this? He'd had hours to try to absorb it and still didn't understand.

She reached for the picture, but instead her fingers curled into a tight fist. "My God, you didn't waste any time. So, who's the baby's mother? Is she someone I know?"

Jared caught her shoulders. Their gazes locked. "You're the mother, Rachel. According to the DNA report, he's our son. *Ours.*"

THE ONLY THING that saved Rachel from losing it then and there was that Jared was obviously lying. He had to be. But what she couldn't figure out was why he was doing something so intentionally cruel.

"Why are you telling me this?" She got up from the bed, snatched up the photograph and shoved it back into the pocket of his black leather jacket. She didn't want even another glimpse of that image of the newborn. "You want to upset me? To get back at me for all the things that went on between us? Then, fine. You've upset me. Now, get out of here."

He caught her hand when she started to pace. "It's the truth, Rachel."

That stopped her in her tracks. There wasn't any hesitation in his voice. Not even a hint. And it was that sheer conviction that had Rachel studying him. What she saw in the depths of those whiskey-colored eyes sent her stomach plummeting to her knees.

"You're not lying?" she mumbled.

But how could that be? She hadn't been with Jared or any other man in over a year. And she darn sure hadn't given birth. *That* she definitely would have remembered.

Jared released the grip he had on her and scrubbed his hands over his face. He groaned softly. "I don't have time to sugarcoat this, so here goes. According to the letter I received late last night, someone claims they stole a frozen fertilized embryo that we'd stored when you were trying to get pregnant. This person says they took it so they could use it to impregnate a surrogate."

It took her several tries just to gather enough breath to speak. "And?"

"And according to them, they succeeded."

Oh God.

Success in this case could mean only one thing. What was left of her composure went south in a hurry. Rachel had no choice but to sit back down on the bed, because her legs gave way.

"There's really a baby? Our baby?"

"According to the letter, yes. Of course, we'd stored several unfertilized eggs as well, so I'm guessing they could have gotten one of those, instead. I just don't know at this point. I've got the people at the fertility clinic checking to verify what's missing, but it doesn't look good. Apparently, frozen embryos aren't a high-theft item so security was pretty lax."

The information was coming at her way too fast. Rachel pressed her hands against her head and tried to concentrate, but it was impossible to absorb something that didn't make sense. "Do you believe it?"

Jared lifted a shoulder, but there was nothing casual about that gesture. And there wasn't a relaxed muscle in his body. "Whoever's behind this included a saliva swab so we could do an independent DNA test. I sent it to the lab before I drove out here, but it'll be a couple of days before we can get the results."

Days. She'd have to wait days to learn the truth. And even then, the test results might not be definitive. After all, someone sinister enough to come up with a plan like this wouldn't hesitate to doctor DNA results.

Still, it wasn't the possibility of doctored DNA results that'd put that strained look in Jared's eyes.

"You must think the child is ours, or you wouldn't be here," Rachel insisted.

He hitched his thumb to his chest. "I'm here because they gave me no choice. All I know at this point is there's *a* child, and Esterman's people have him."

"Yes." It sickened her to know that a man like Esterman held the fate of a baby in his hands. The man was a killer. "But why would he do something like this?"

The moment the question left her mouth, Rachel knew why. God. She knew. "It's because of my testimony, isn't it?"

Jared nodded. "They want you to lie this afternoon when you take the stand, to exonerate Esterman. If you don't, they say they'll kill the baby."

The adrenaline and the emotions slammed into her like a fist. She fought to keep her breath level. But lost that battle. Rachel tried to remind herself that it might not even be true. The photo and the DNA report could be fakes. It was possible this was all just a ploy to stop her from putting a killer away for the rest of his life.

But it didn't feel like a ploy.

It felt as if her child was in horrible danger.

"Now that you know, it's decision time, Rachel. I could force you to go with me, but in the end I'll need your cooperation."

Cooperation? She wasn't sure she could even move. A dozen emotions assaulted her. None good. So many doubts. So much confusion.

A baby. God, *a baby*.

"Rachel, are you sure you're all right?" Detective Miller called out.

"Don't open the door," Jared whispered.

He extracted a small tool kit from his pocket, went to the window and proceeded to disarm the security system. That explained why he was wearing a jacket on a muggy spring day. He had to conceal heaven-knows-what to help them escape.

But the real question was—did she want to escape?

"Convince her to give us some time alone," Jared instructed. "Lots of time. We'll need it if you're leaving with me."

Rachel nodded, somehow. And somehow she managed to get off the bed. She made it to the door, praying her voice wouldn't break.

"I'm okay," she lied. "Jared will be staying until we leave for the courthouse."

The silence on the other side of the door didn't do much to settle Rachel's raw, tangled nerves. It was obvious Jared didn't want either of the other officers involved in this, and Rachel would go along with him on that.

For now.

But there were still too many questions that needed answers before she'd leave with him.

"Maybe I should call Captain Thornton?" Miller suggested. "I mean, just so she'll know Lieutenant Dillard is here visiting you."

Rachel understood the implications of that. And they weren't good implications. Miller wasn't a fool and she no doubt suspected something was wrong.

She looked over her shoulder at Jared. He merely shook his head and continued to work on the window.

"No need to call anyone." Rachel pulled in a long breath so she could finish. "I just want to, um, talk things out with Jared."

Another pause. Rachel pressed her forehead against the door and waited. She really didn't want to speculate what would happen if Detective Miller decided to make that call.

"Okay. Whatever you say, Rachel. But I'll stay put right out here in the hall. Just yell if you need me."

Oh, she would do that. Too bad it might become necessary. Because she didn't know if she could even trust Jared. Their last months together hadn't exactly fostered a trusting relationship. There'd been too many incidents where they'd frozen each other out. Along with that had come the bitter feelings and the accusations. He definitely wasn't the same person she'd vowed to love, honor and cherish five years ago.

But then, neither was she.

During their separation, they'd grown as far apart as two people could get. Heck, they hadn't even contacted each other the entire time she'd been at the ranch house. Yet here he was, right back in her life.

Jared put his tool kit away and eased open the window. The morning breeze stirred the curtains when he shoved out the screen. No alarms went off, which meant he'd successfully deactivated the system.

"If you're doing this, we have to leave now," Jared insisted.

But Rachel held her ground. "And then what?"

Obviously not pleased with her lack of cooperation, he mumbled some profanity under his breath. "I need to take you someplace safe so you won't have to testify. The courts will almost certainly ask for another trial delay while they try to locate you. In the meantime, we find this child and get him out of danger."

It was a simple plan. Also a vague one. And it had holes in it the size of the Alamo.

"You didn't turn this over to the police," Rachel pointed out. "Why?"

This was one of those times she wished she didn't know Jared so well. His mouth tightened. A muscle stirred in his firm jaw. And a sickening feeling crawled down her spine before he even answered.

"The person who wrote that letter said the baby would die if we told the cops, and I'm pretty sure there's a leak in the department. A big one from a person who can do lots of damage if he puts his mind to it. I'll give you the details once we're out of here."

Great. Just great. Her life had just been turned upside down and inside out. Somewhere out there, a child—maybe their child—was possibly in grave danger, and they couldn't even go to the police.

Rachel debated and wished like the devil that she had more time to figure out what to do. This could easily be construed as the point of no return. Once she went out that window, she would essentially be on the run. A fugitive. But if she stayed and told the truth to convict a killer, then a child might die.

Jared helped her decision along. "Every minute we waste here, we could be using to find the baby."

He was right, of course—about that particular argument, anyway. She couldn't be sure about anything else.

However, when Jared gripped her arm, Rachel didn't argue. Didn't take a step back. She climbed out into the yard with him. Then she prayed, hoping this wasn't the biggest mistake of her life.

Jared didn't give her time to dwell on her doubts. He kept low, his gaze darting all around. He led her to the side of the house, toward the detached garage.

"We're taking one of the detective's cars?" Rachel whispered.

"No. But I need a distraction."

Looping his arm around her waist, he ducked behind some thick shrubs. He paused a moment and checked out the yard before he continued to the side door of the garage. From the corner of her eye, Rachel saw him try to turn the knob.

It was locked.

Other than one single harsh word of profanity, he said nothing. Instead, he rammed his shoulder into it, but when that didn't budge it, he snatched the tiny tool kit from his pocket and got to work picking the lock.

Rachel's gaze whipped back to the open window where they'd escaped. No sign of the officers. Yet. But they'd come. After all, it was their job to get her to the courthouse. Once they realized she wasn't in the bedroom, the search would be on.

For months, she'd prepared herself for that testimony, and for its aftermath. A divorce. A new life. A new identity. Out with the old and in with the new. But instead of putting the undercover investigation and her past behind her, she was apparently about to leap headfirst back into it.

God.

Was she doing the right thing? Maybe there was some other way to save the child. Some way that didn't involve them going on the run.

Rachel heard the sound at the exact moment that Jared apparently did. Footsteps. Some movement along the driveway on the side of the house. He reacted quickly. Jared shoved her behind him and pressed her against the wall of the garage.

She waited. And listened. Even over the thuds of her own heartbeat, Rachel clearly heard the footsteps on the cement. They were hardly more than whispers, but it wasn't difficult to tell where they were headed.

Right toward them.

It was probably Detective Smith doing a routine check of the grounds, but if he saw them, there'd be nothing routine about his reaction.

Jared turned, facing her, and he went back to picking the lock. She saw the intense focus in his eyes. Felt his breath brush against her cheek. Felt the heat of his body.

But she also felt his shoulder holster, and his weapon.

That didn't do much to steady her heart. Thank God he hadn't drawn it, but he probably would if that was the only way they could get out of there.

The footsteps suddenly stopped. She'd seen Smith do a check of grounds dozens of times and knew he was thorough. He'd no doubt be coming around the side of the garage very soon. Too soon. She and Jared needed to get inside, or Smith would certainly see them.

The lock finally gave way, and Jared pushed her inside and quickly followed. There were two cars parked in the dark, cramped space. He opened the door on the one nearest them and retrieved the remote for the garage.

"Come on," Jared whispered. But he didn't use the remote. He opened the side door again and peered out.

"Rachel?" she heard Detective Miller call out, the sound coming through the open window of her bedroom. But it wasn't the only sound. The officer soon began to pound on the door. "Open up. I want to make sure you're all right in there."

Jared glanced over his shoulder at her and put his finger to his mouth in a stay-quiet gesture. He led her out of the garage, staying behind the shrubs, and they made it to the side of the house. Only then did he lean back around the corner and press the button on the remote opener.

The noise started almost immediately as the metal door began to lift. Jared didn't waste any time. He tossed down the remote, latched onto her and got her moving toward the front of the house where he'd parked.

Smith shouted something to Miller, and a second later, Rachel heard the back door slam. The diversion had worked.

Well, maybe.

Once the officers verified that both of their vehicles were in the garage, they'd start looking elsewhere.

Jared opened the door on the driver side of his car and pushed her through to the passenger seat. He peeled off his jacket, tossing it on the seat. Probably so he'd have better access to his shoulder holster.

Not a comforting thought.

The key was already in the ignition, and he wasted no time starting it.

Rachel caught a glimpse of Miller and Smith as they raced around the side of the house toward them. Both had their weapons drawn and ready. That didn't deter Jared.

"Get down, Rachel," he ordered.

He gunned the engine and headed for the road.

Chapter Two

Jared shot past Miller and Smith and sped along the gravel road in front of the house. His best chance was to make it to the highway and try to outrun the two cops. And maybe, just maybe, those Texas Rangers at the checkpoint wouldn't shoot first and ask questions later.

Of course, escape from the safe house was just the first hurdle. He didn't want to speculate how many hurdles they had ahead of them after that.

Or what those hurdles might be.

Even some serious detective work and a fair amount luck might not be enough to help them find the child—and stay ahead of danger.

"Are they following us?" Rachel asked.

Jared glanced in the side and rearview mirrors. "Not yet."

But he quickly had to amend that. The moment

the words left his mouth, he saw the dark gray car barrel out of the garage, coming right after them.

"They're behind us," he said. "Stay down. The tires are bullet resistant, but they might try to shoot them out anyway."

"Oh God." She mumbled another curse under her breath. "What have we gotten ourselves into?"

He was asking himself the same thing. Jared tried not to think beyond saving this child that *might* be theirs. But even if they managed to get the baby out of harm's way and put Esterman behind bars, there would be consequences.

Huge ones.

After all, he was essentially kidnapping his soon-to-be ex-wife so he could obstruct justice. The department certainly wasn't going to see that in a favorable light, no matter how good his intentions. When this was over, he'd have some serious explaining to do.

Jared kept his eyes on the zigzagging road and spotted the Rangers' checkpoint station just ahead. Both men were there. Waiting. The detectives must have alerted them, because the Rangers had angled their car to create a roadblock.

Without slowing down, Jared veered around them, using every inch of the grassy shoulder, and raced past the checkpoint. As he'd figured they would do, the Rangers jumped into their vehicle and followed in pursuit. They wouldn't just give up and let him leave the area with Rachel.

"What now?" she asked.

She lifted her head and looked out the side mirror. Jared pushed her right back down. If the officers tried to shoot out the tires and missed, he didn't want Rachel to become the victim of "friendly" fire.

Rachel didn't exactly cooperate. The minute his hand was off her shoulder, she slipped right back up in the seat and pinned her gaze to the mirror, and their pursuers. From her soft gasp, she obviously knew things weren't going well.

He took the next curve, and the other cars made the turn along with him. And worse. Jared saw the detectives drop back so the Rangers could overtake them. One of the Rangers leaned out of the window and aimed his weapon at the tires.

Hell.

Jared pushed Rachel down in the seat again. He definitely didn't want her to get a good look at that rifle. With her fear of firearms, she might have a panic attack. There wasn't time for that.

He didn't slow down. Jared kept the pressure on the accelerator and snaked over both lanes so the tires wouldn't be such easy targets. Unfortunately, that didn't protect them from a quick jab of Murphy's Law.

"Hang on," Jared warned.

At seemingly a snail's pace, an old beat-up truck hauling a flatbed of hay pulled out from a side road and directly into their path. He managed to swerve around it. Barely. The car jerked to the right when he clipped the ditch. Jared corrected and then corrected again so he wouldn't broadside a tree.

He heard the sound of metal scraping and buckling and saw the cause of that noise in his rearview mirror. The Rangers and detectives hadn't been so lucky in avoiding an accident.

They'd sideswiped each other to avoid the truck, and the impact had sent both cars careering into a waist-high ditch. Everyone looked unharmed, but their vehicles were temporarily out of commission. It'd probably take a tow truck to get them back on the road.

Jared didn't waste any time. He stomped on the accelerator and got them out of there.

"We can't follow the highway," he said.

He sped toward the farm road that he'd already checked out. By his estimation, it would take five minutes to get there and another five minutes to start working their way through the maze of back roads that would eventually lead them to the cabin.

"They'll set up blocks to find us."

When she didn't respond, Jared glanced at her. Rachel was no longer sitting low in the seat. Nor did she have her attention focused on the accident behind them. Rather, she was looking at the envelope and the photograph that had fallen out of his jacket pocket.

"Who is she?" Rachel asked.

The picture lay between them. The gruesome image that he hadn't wanted Rachel to see.

Jared checked the mirror again to make sure they weren't being followed. They weren't, but it wouldn't stay that way for long. He hadn't intended to get into an explanation like this until they were someplace safe. Of course, he didn't have a clue when that would be.

He tried to put the picture of the dead woman back into the envelope, but Rachel pushed his hand away.

"Esterman's people sent this to you, didn't they." Rachel's voice was ragged, laced with nerves and adrenaline, but there was fire there as well.

Jared knew exactly how she felt. He'd had the same reaction the first time he saw it. It wasn't any easier the second time around. "Yeah. It was in the envelope with the letter and the photo of the baby."

He debated how much more he should tell her, but the debate didn't last long. This was a critical piece of information that he couldn't keep from Rachel. She'd risked as much as he had by leaving the safe house. Besides, he needed her cooperation, and this unfortunately might do it.

"I computer-matched that photo to the one in her

police record,'' Jared explained. ''Her name is Sasha Young. She did time for forgery, and she's—''

''The surrogate mother,'' Rachel finished. ''The woman who supposedly gave birth to our child.'' She paused and moistened her lips. ''They murdered her?''

Oh, man. This wasn't an easy thing to discuss with Rachel. If the people behind this would kill a young woman, they probably wouldn't hesitate to kill again. But then, Rachel must have come to that same conclusion. If she hadn't truly thought a child was in danger, she wouldn't have climbed out that window with him.

''It appears they murdered her,'' Jared admitted.

She narrowed her eyes. ''*Appears?* That's twice you've used that word today, and it's starting to annoy me. Cut the doublespeak, Jared. Is she dead, or is this a doctored photo to scare us into doing what Esterman wants?''

If he hadn't been so concerned over what they were about to face, he might have smiled. Might have. Here, he'd expected the news to send Rachel into a near panic. And it no doubt had. But even so, she was holding herself together—for now, anyway. However, they weren't even close to finishing this.

''I don't know if she's really dead,'' he admitted. ''I checked the morgue, and there's no Jane Doe fitting her description, but that doesn't mean anything.

They could have taken that picture and then disposed of the body so that it wouldn't be found—ever.''

''Yes.'' Rachel took a deep breath, and another, and rested her head against the seat.

''I know this isn't easy, and I'm sorry.'' That picture probably reminded her of her own murdered parents. It was the main reason Jared hadn't been eager to show it to her.

Her head whipped up. ''My God, your mother and your sister. Esterman might go after them—''

''I've already taken care of it. I sent Karen and Mom on a little trip out of state this morning. With bodyguards. They'll be fine.''

At least, Jared hoped they would be. He was thankful that his family had gone willingly into hiding. Of course, he hadn't given them much of a choice. Jared was sure the only reason Esterman hadn't thought to use them sooner was that Rachel and he had been separated. If Esterman had believed for one minute that he could get to Rachel through them, they would have become his first choice of targets.

''They must be terrified,'' Rachel concluded.

Yep. But Jared wasn't about to confirm it. It would only push their feelings of panic up a notch. ''They know I'll defuse this situation with Esterman as fast as I can.''

She glanced at him. Not exactly a vote of confidence. Rachel shook her head. "After the cops asked me to spy on Esterman, I learned the horrible things that he's capable of doing. Well, at least I thought I had. But this…God, this. I didn't know anyone could come up with something so sinister. And to think I used to work for this man. Heck, I used to believe we were friends."

Friends. Oh yeah. Jared had caught wind of some of that. When things had been at the worst in their marriage, Rachel had mentioned something about having a few long talks with her boss.

That still didn't set well with him.

Not just for the obvious personal reasons, either. It likely meant that Esterman knew some of the details of Rachel's and his breakup. If the man knew that, then he was also aware of how much Rachel desperately wanted a child. Esterman must have used that information when he put this plan together.

And he'd come after her with a vengeance.

"I don't regret spying on him," she continued several moments later. "And I don't regret turning over the information to police. Money laundering. Murder for hire. All under the guise of a respectable accounting firm." Rachel placed the photo in the envelope and neatly tucked it back into his jacket pocket. "But I do regret that the investigation brought things to this point."

So did he. And even after hours of thinking of

little else, he just hadn't come up with a way to fight Esterman. But then, Esterman had had a year to come up with his plan to stop Rachel from testifying. Jared had had just hours, and precious few of those.

Jared turned onto the little-used farm road and checked his mirror again. Still no sign of any Rangers or cops, but they had almost certainly called for backup. By now, peace officers all over the area would be responding. His captain would have been alerted—and maybe even the city officials. It put a hard knot in his stomach to know that for the first time in his life he was on the other side of the law.

"How long do you think we have before they find us?" she asked.

Probably not long enough. But he kept that to himself. Best to dwell on the things they did have some control over.

"I don't know, but we start by getting out of sight," he explained. "Then, we find the baby so you can testify. Before I came to get you, I called the prison where Sasha Young was an inmate. The warden's administrative assistant told me that she had a frequent visitor, a man named Aaron Merkens. I've already located him and arranged a meeting for tonight."

"Tonight," she repeated on a heavy sigh.

Jared understood that sigh all too well. Tonight was still hours away, and a lot could happen between now and then. The two bodyguards were after them. The Rangers. Maybe even his own fellow officers. Added to that, there was a storm brewing. The thick sludge-colored cloud looked ready to burst wide open, and that would certainly put a damper on his driving like a bat out of hell.

But those things were only part of their problem. He and Rachel couldn't go far since they needed to be in San Antonio for that meeting with Aaron Merkens. As meetings went, that one was critical. Merkens might be able to tell them the location of the baby. The flip side was that he might lead them straight into a trap.

It was definitely a rock and a hard place kind of situation.

Yet, there was nothing Jared could do about it. He had to meet with the man. He had to figure out where to start looking. But first and foremost, he had to make sure that he and Rachel weren't captured.

As much as he hated to admit it even to himself, they and they alone were the baby's only chance for survival.

CLARENCE ESTERMAN CALMLY leaned back in the stiff prison-gray chair and stared through the thick, dingy glass at his employee. Gerald Anderson was on a roll, his words fluid. His voice strong and steady. But Clarence looked past that news-at-five veneer and saw a man who was scared spitless of being the messenger for this particular communiqué.

"I'm listening," Clarence assured him when Gerald paused and gulped down some water.

But there was no reason for Clarence to listen too carefully. The oily beads of sweat over Gerald's ample upper lip said it all. Someone had screwed up badly enough that it had warranted a visit from his personal assistant and security specialist.

That did not please him.

There were only two things he hated more than receiving bad news: the stench of the jail and the woman responsible for putting him there. Make that three—he could add yet another thing to his hate list. Lieutenant Jared Dillard.

"Our friend was supposed to have been observed 24/7. No exceptions." Even though he whispered that little reminder, Clarence enunciated each word into the offensive-smelling phone that he was forced to use. He'd already bribed the guards to make sure the conversation wasn't being monitored, but he still chose his words carefully. "Please tell me why that didn't happen."

Gerald made a vague who-knows motion with his hand. "He managed to, uh, shake the observer. I guess he's better at that than we thought he'd be."

"He's very good at what he does," Clarence said calmly. "Lots of citations and plaques for his I-love-me wall. But everyone knew that before we ever made him our messenger boy. So, if I take that 'he's very good' information to the most obvious conclusion, then everyone, including you and the observer, should have anticipated that he'd try to stop us from keeping tabs on him.''

No more news-at-five demeanor. The transformation he saw in Gerald was something immediate and akin to a deer crashing straight into the headlights of a fully loaded semi with its pedal to the metal.

''We'll find him'' was Gerald's comeback after he'd guzzled down more water.

''Oh, I have no doubt of that, not with what I pay you. And when you do locate him, you'll remind him of the little package we have. That should help him get his priorities back on track. You'll also inform him that he's deeply pissed me off with this little evasion tactic.''

Gerald nodded, as Clarence had known he would do. ''Absolutely.''

But that wasn't enough. Not when his freedom and his life were at stake.

''Shake things up a little,'' Clarence continued. He ignored the guard's impatient request for him to hurry his visit. ''I want our mutual friend to realize how important it is that we have his cooperation.''

Gerald leaned forward until his nose was practically against the glass. "You're not saying what I think you're saying…"

Clarence leaned forward as well, but unlike Gerald, he was absolutely certain there wasn't a trace of fear or concern in his baby blues.

"I merely want him…surprised," Clarence explained. He wasn't totally opposed to killing a cop, but he wasn't giving up on getting Dillard's help in bringing in Rachel. "Have I mentioned that someone very close to him has a fear of guns? A childhood trauma. Something about witnessing her parents' murders. Use that."

Gerald shook his head. "How?"

Clarence slowly brought his teeth together, and it took a moment to unclench them. It was hard to maintain composure when dealing with a certifiable moron. Too bad he needed this particular moron.

For a little while longer, anyway.

"Educate her the hard way, Gerald. Send her running from her estranged husband, and she will run right where we want her."

"And if she doesn't?"

Clarence didn't bother answering that. He had no doubt whatsoever that Rachel would cooperate once the truth sank in about the baby. Simply put, the child was what mattered most to her. Not her super-cop estranged husband that she hadn't bothered to contact in over a year. Not her warped sense of devotion to be a do-gooder for the sake of society.

The baby was Rachel Dillard's Achilles' heel.

And he would use it to break her.

Clarence placed the phone back on the wall, knowing that Gerald would do what he had been told. Hopefully, this time he'd manage it without the mistakes. Of course, Clarence did have a margin for error.

All seven pounds and three ounces of him.

It would be interesting to watch Rachel beg for the child's life.

Chapter Three

Rachel looked out through the rain-streaked windshield and spotted the picturesque log cabin. It was nestled in a thick grove of moss-strewn oaks, making it difficult to see from the road.

Difficult, but certainly not impossible.

And that explained why Jared parked the car at the back of the cabin where it would be out of sight.

"This place belongs to a friend," Jared explained as they made a dash for the back porch. "We can use it as long as necessary."

Rachel wondered if the friend was a man or a woman, but she quickly pushed that question aside. His relationships, personal or otherwise, were no longer any of her business. After all, she and Jared had called it quits months ago. He was a healthy, red-blooded, thirty-two-year-old male, and it was likely—very likely—that he'd been seeing other women.

While the rain pelted them and the lightning slashed across the sky, Jared fished a key out of his pocket and unlocked the door. The place was musky but dry, and a lot larger than it looked from the outside.

Well, sort of.

The combined living and kitchen area was large enough to accommodate two people, but what Rachel didn't see was a separate bedroom. The double bed tucked away in the corner seemed to be the sum total of the sleeping quarters. Hopefully, they wouldn't have to spend the night.

"We'll be safe here until it's time to meet Aaron Merkens?" she asked.

"We should be." After Jared entered the code on the wall pad to disarm the security system, he grabbed a towel from the closet near the door and tossed it to her. "I figure you're the safest woman in America right now. Esterman will do just about anything to keep you alive. You're his get-out-jail-free card. Or so he thinks."

Yes. But her supposed safety came at a huge price. Esterman would only want her alive as long as she could be of service to him.

All bets were off after that.

"I asked if *we* would be safe," Rachel clarified. She watched as he lifted a laptop from the top shelf of the closet and set it on the pine table. "That plural pronoun included you."

With an almost amused look on his face, he brushed past her so he could plug the modem line into the phone jack on the wall. She caught his scent. The wet leather of his jacket. Faint traces of soap.

He still used the same shampoo.

It had always reminded her of the sea. And sex. But then a lot of things about Jared still reminded her of sex.

He was so unlike the other guys she'd dated in college. No comparison really. He was basically a grown-up bad boy who'd won his share of fights, some with his fists. The tiny scar on his chin and the other on the edge of his right eyebrow were evidence of that.

Like the rest of him, his hair was a bit untamed, a little too long—with a natural style that fit his personality to a tee. No glossy polish. No pretenses. Just a man who had a unique way of reminding her that she was very glad indeed to be a woman.

Even now, with all the uncertainty of the moment, she still had the same reaction to Jared that she usually did. Much to her disgust, he pretty much stole her breath. God knows how many times that had happened, so she couldn't blame it on the adrenaline. All he had to do was walk into a room and she melted into a puddle of...something.

Something that Rachel quickly pushed aside.

Those days of lust and great sex were over. They were on the brink of a divorce and their lives were in turmoil. This wasn't the time for the-way-we-were musings.

"I appreciate the plural pronoun, and the concern for my safety," Jared commented. "But I seriously doubt Esterman wants to tangle with me."

Rachel wasn't so sure. Tangling seemed to be something that didn't intimidate Clarence Esterman, and that was only one of the reasons why the thought of his going free chilled her to the bone.

She checked the time. It was nearly twelve-thirty. In a half an hour she was supposed to be on the stand to testify about all the incriminating documents and memos she'd observed her boss shredding. Since there were no other witnesses, she was essentially the prosecution's case. Yet, here she was, in a remote cabin at least thirty miles from the courthouse. The district attorney's office and dozens of other people were probably in an uproar by now.

"I can build a fire if you want to dry off," Jared offered.

"No thanks." Despite the rain, the room was muggy and warm, which wasn't unusual for a Texas spring afternoon. However, that combined with the spent adrenaline was making her feel woozy. She definitely needed a clear head for the things they

were about to face. "I'd rather try to figure out how
we're going to find the baby."

The sooner that happened, the sooner she could
take the stand. And the sooner she'd know if *the*
baby was actually *their* baby. Rachel didn't want to
think beyond that. One step at a time was all she
could handle right now.

He draped his jacket over the back of a chair, the
drops of rain sliding off it and spattering onto the
hardwood floor. "Like I told you in the car, I'm hoping Aaron Merkens can give us a starting point."

Yes. That would prevent them from having to take
the needle-in-a-haystack approach, but it still wasn't
very reassuring. After all, Sasha Young had been in
prison, and Merkens was her friend.

"You think you can trust him?"

"No way in hell."

She almost wished Jared had hesitated. The fact
that he hadn't meant the meeting that was supposed
to take place in seven hours might just be a trap.

Maybe Esterman had known they'd find Merkens
and try to get information from him. And if Esterman
had known that, then he also could have arranged for
the cops to be there to take her back into protective
custody.

Talk about the ultimate irony. When it came to her
testimony, Esterman and the cops were now on the
same side. Both would do just about anything to

get her to take the stand. One, however, wanted her to lie.

With his back to her, Jared peeled off his wet shirt and hung it over one of the other chairs to dry. "Remember Mason Tanner, the P.I. I've used for some of my cases?"

"Sure." When she and Jared were still together, Turner came to the house a couple of times. "What about him?"

"He's helping us out. A lot. I'm having him check out the park where we're meeting Merkens, and he'll try to make sure it's safe. I can't leave you here by yourself. You'll have to come with me."

Rachel hadn't considered staying behind to be an option, anyway. As difficult as it was to be around Jared, it would have been impossible to do this solo.

"What about this leak in the department you mentioned earlier?" she asked, trying not to look directly at him. It seemed a little too intimate to be so close to him while he was half naked. Instead, she straightened the stack of old magazines in the center of the table.

It didn't help.

Her body still knew he was half naked.

"A couple of weeks ago someone put a tap on my phone at work." He extracted the envelope from his jacket and tossed it next to the magazines. "Then I caught this officer over in homicide, Sergeant Colby

Meredith, trying to access some security files. Files that would have told him the location of the safe house where you were staying.''

''Sweet heaven.'' Rachel had never heard Esterman mention this particular person, but he had a lot of people on his payroll. ''You confronted Meredith?''

''Sure did. He only recently transferred in from Austin, so he covered for himself by saying he wasn't familiar with the files and accidentally typed in the wrong code. I didn't believe him for a minute, so I've been watching him. But I figure Esterman put Meredith in place to find you so he could have one of his hired goons personally deliver the news about the baby. When Meredith wasn't successful, Esterman had no choice but to use me as a middleman.''

Of course. They probably hadn't wanted to involve Jared since he was a cop, but he was one of the few people who could get to her. That one little detail had embroiled him in all of this.

He turned to type something on the keyboard, and Rachel saw the scar. An angry slice across his chest, just below his heart. She actually took a step back, to put some distance between her and that brutal reminder of what had happened nearly eighteen months earlier.

''Pretty disgusting, huh?'' she heard him say.

Only then did Rachel realize she'd been staring at his chest.

Unable to answer him, she merely shook her head. *Disgusting* wasn't the right word. More like *distressing*. The injury had nearly killed him. In fact, the doctors told her that his heart had stopped beating while he was in surgery.

Jared shrugged and went to the closet. He grabbed two T-shirts off hangers, slipped on one and handed the other one to her. "They tell me it'll fade with time."

The scar would, yes. The memory of it wouldn't. Nor would the rift it had caused between them.

In the end, the event that had caused that scar had also cost them their marriage. For Rachel, it had been easier to fall out of love with Jared than to risk another nightmare like that. She'd had enough nightmares to last a lifetime.

Rachel changed her shirt in the tiny bathroom and hung the other up to dry. She turned to leave, but first made the mistake of glancing in the mirror. No makeup. Her hair was soaking wet. She was much too pale. She looked even worse than she felt— something she hadn't thought possible.

"We're connected to the Internet," Jared called out. "Think you can try to find out some information about Sasha Young's last known address?"

"I'll try." Glad that she could do something to get

her mind off their situation, Rachel went back into the room and took the seat in front of the computer.

Jared moved the envelope closer to her, and she noticed the address written on the outside. ''I got that from Aaron Merkens,'' he explained. ''It's supposedly a rental house on the south side of town, but it could be bogus. There was no phone listing for it. While you're doing that, I need to call Tanner.''

Jared took out his cell phone and walked into the kitchen to make his call. Rachel didn't waste any time. She used some of her CPA knowledge and located the real estate tax records for the county. With any luck, the actual owner of the property would be listed.

While she waited for the file to load, she glanced at the envelope. She already knew it contained the photos of the dead woman and the baby, but she was almost afraid to find out what other surprises it held—especially since they were dealing with Esterman here.

Trying to ignore the envelope, Rachel quickly scanned the tax information on the screen, but it wasn't good news. The owner of the rental property was a corporation. Probably a dummy company at that. If Esterman owned the house, he was too smart not to bury that information under layers of paperwork.

She fed in the next search to try to find out more information about the corporation, while toying with the flap on the envelope. Rachel tried to talk herself out of opening it, but even knowing that the contents could break her heart, she couldn't stop herself. The first thing she saw when she glanced inside was the photo of the baby.

It took her a moment just to find her breath and longer to steady it. As if it were fragile and might shatter in her hand, she lifted it out and placed it neatly on the table next to the computer. She hadn't really looked at the image when Jared tried to hand it to her in the bedroom at the safe house, but she studied it now.

The tiny round face was perfect. Beautiful. A delicate mouth. A spattering of bronze-colored hair on his head. The color of Jared's hair. Of course, that meant nothing. Lots of babies had brown hair.

He could be anyone's child. Anyone's. And Esterman could be using him the same way he'd used dozens of other people over the three years she'd worked for him. Still, Rachel couldn't seem to take her gaze off that precious little face.

His eyes were closed in what appeared to be a peaceful sleep. She prayed that it was indeed peaceful, and that he had no comprehension whatsoever of the danger he was in.

God.

He was in danger because Esterman had chosen to use him as a pawn in a very sick game.

But was this her baby?

Was this the child she'd desperately wanted but had given up hope of ever having?

The memories of her infertility blended together with the tormenting thoughts of the baby. Looking back on it, Jared had never seemed as committed to having a child as she had. He hadn't objected. Not really. But then, he hadn't poured his whole heart into it, either. He'd proven that when he refused to let her use the fertilized embryos immediately after they separated. He hadn't wanted to bring a child into a broken relationship.

Or so he said.

At the time, his steadfast refusal had felt like the ultimate slap in the face. It still did. If she hadn't gotten involved with the undercover investigation into Esterman's wrongdoings, she almost certainly would have pursued the issue in court. That was the only reason the embryos still had been in storage. So, in a way it was her fault that Esterman had been able to carry things through to this point.

She touched the photograph again, running her fingertips over the baby's mouth. His lips were pursed slightly as if he'd just had a bottle. That brought on another wave of fear and panic. Were they feeding him? Was there anyone to hold him when he cried?

Rachel wasn't even aware that she was crying until she felt a tear slide down her cheek. More followed, and though she tried to choke it back, the sound of her sob cut through the room.

Jared was suddenly there, next to her. He didn't reach out for her. Thank God—she didn't think she could handle that right now.

"I'm sorry," Rachel whispered, shaking her head. "I tried to hold it together."

"No apology necessary." He slid his hands into the pockets of his jeans and rocked back on his heels. "I know this isn't easy for you."

"Still, the tears won't help. They never do." She swiped the rest of them away. "You're the only man who's ever seen me cry. You know that?"

"Women tell me that all the time." Jared smiled. "I'm not sure it's a compliment."

It was the right thing to say. A lighthearted and typical Jared comeback to diffuse an otherwise tense moment. Rachel wanted to give in to it, to sit there and let him comfort her. But she couldn't. If she took that kind of comfort from him, it would be too easy to fall back into the same old patterns.

Jared was still a cop. A cop who put duty above anything else, including his own life.

And that would always be there between them.

Rachel stifled the rest of her tears and returned to the computer. But Jared didn't move. He stood there staring down at her. When she lifted her gaze to his, she saw that his immobility wasn't just because of her tearful reaction to the photo.

"Did you get through to Tanner?" she asked.

Jared nodded. "We couldn't talk long. He had to make another call."

"What's wrong?" Rachel held her breath and waited for an explanation.

"Tanner just told me that the cops found Sasha Young's body a couple of hours ago."

"Oh." It hit Rachel a lot harder than she would have thought it would, and the breath swooshed out of her. Moments earlier, Sasha Young had been simply a possibility. A potential piece of a puzzle.

"She was murdered," Jared continued. "Strangled. Her body was dumped in the Guadalupe River, but some fisherman spotted it and called the cops."

As horrible as that was, Rachel knew he wasn't finished. There was more. "And?"

"Tanner knows the medical examiner, so he got the guy to give him a preliminary report. Miss Young recently had a C-section." Jared looked her straight in the eye. "He estimates the surgery was done about a week ago."

A week. The timing was perfect. The pieces were starting to come together—with one horrible, inevitable conclusion. Esterman's plan was real. Not some hoax meant to scare her into cooperating.

There was indeed a child.

Somewhere.

And he was in terrible danger.

Chapter Four

He listened while Mason Tanner fleshed out the news he'd just delivered, but Jared seriously doubted the fleshing out would make it any more palatable.

Basically, it sucked.

"Your captain wasn't pleased when I told her I didn't know where you were," Tanner continued. "I guess she figured we'd be in touch, and that I'd try to talk some sense into you. Well, consider yourself talked to, because I'm on your side all the way. I don't think you have a choice about what you're doing right now."

"Thanks," Jared mumbled. But he didn't need anyone, including his friend, to reiterate the fact that his options were slim and none. He was painfully aware of it.

"So Captain Thornton basically thinks I've kidnapped Rachel?" Jared asked Tanner.

That garnered Rachel's attention. Jared saw her

fingers still on the keyboard, and she looked up from the screen. Her left eyebrow arched questioningly. She probably wanted to know how he felt about that.

In other words, a rhetorical question.

Jared decided it was a good time to stare out the window and finish his conversation.

"Have they made it official?" Jared asked, lowering his voice. "Is there an APB or anything else I should be aware of?"

"No. Not as of an hour ago, anyway—but the cops are *quietly* looking for you. The chief of police apparently isn't too eager to put out an APB on one of the department's most decorated officers. Face it, Jared, you're the Dudley Do-Right poster child for SAPD."

Jared shook his head and silently cursed Tanner's sarcasm. "And they think their poster child has gone skydiving off the deep end but that I'll soon come to my senses?"

"Something like that. A temporary insanity kind of thing brought on by the upcoming divorce and the ordeal that Rachel's been through."

The affirmation had his throat tightening. Hell. He'd known all along that it could come to this. His reputation would basically be trashed. Perhaps along with his career. A career he'd spent twelve long years building.

Esterman couldn't have planned it any better. In

one swoop, the man had hit both him and Rachel where it hurt the most.

The baby and the badge.

Jared didn't even want to guess what else Esterman had in store for them. Round one sure wasn't going that well.

"What about the meeting with Merkens?" Jared asked, forcing his attention back to the matter at hand. He couldn't dwell on things he couldn't fix, and at the moment his reputation at headquarters was well out of the repairable mode. He had to solve this case before he could even start damage control. "Is that a go?"

"Sure, but you know there's no way I can guarantee that either the location or Merkens will be safe. Too many variables and too much open space."

"I know. I didn't pick the location, and I wasn't asking for miracles. I just don't want to be ambushed by Esterman's men before I step out of the car."

"I'll do my best. My advice—watch your back. And your front."

Oh, he would do that. But Jared wasn't certain that'd be enough.

Jared ended the call and slipped his phone back into his jacket pocket. "Good news," he told Rachel. Best to try to sound optimistic even if there wasn't squat to be optimistic about. "They delayed the trial to give the prosecution a chance to find you."

She didn't say anything for several moments. "The cops are after you?"

It really wasn't a good time for her to ask that. And maybe it was his imagination, or else the massive amount of baggage between them, but Jared heard the old disapproval in her tone. Not that he needed more, but it fueled his frustration and put him on the defensive.

"I still have my badge," he said quickly. "I'm still a cop."

She made a sound that could have meant anything, or nothing. Unfortunately, it felt like *something*.

"Look, I know you don't approve of what I do, Rachel, but if you don't mind, I'd rather skip the cold shoulder and lecture this afternoon. I've already got enough to deal with here without rehashing the past."

She issued a dismissive glance and calmly turned her attention back to the computer screen. "Thanks for that reminder, Jared." He couldn't help but notice that she pressed the keys a little harder than required. "I was starting to have a few lustful thoughts about you, but I'm sure that'll fix the problem."

Jared had already geared up to move on to the next subject—the meeting with Merkens—but then her comment sank in.

"Lustful thoughts?" he repeated.

Rachel nodded. "You know, as in those thoughts dealing with lust?"

Nope. He hadn't misunderstood her. It was a very succinct and sarcastic answer. Now, the question was—how should he respond? *Should* he respond?

Rachel helped him along with his decision. Well, in a roundabout sort of way. She didn't even blink. But she did hike up her chin and pull the ice-princess act that he pretty much hated. And she knew it, too. He could tell by the almost smug glint in her eye.

"Believe me, that wasn't the clarification I was looking for," he insisted. "What I meant was…" Jared stopped and rethought the question that had been about to fly out of his mouth. There was a fine line between a request for information and an idiotic remark. Best to go for the direct approach. "What the hell are you saying, anyway?"

She shrugged. "I don't have Alzheimer's, Jared. I know how good we once were in bed."

So did he. And for some reason those memories had gotten a lot more vivid since he'd seen her at the safe house.

He could still remember the taste of her.

Damn it.

"But I also recall what sent us running in opposite directions," she continued. Rachel moved the envelope, aligning it with the table edge. "You nearly getting killed. Me whining to you every few minutes about you nearly getting killed. Both of us resenting it. I'm sure neither of us wants to go back there again. Right?''

''Right. I guess.''

Actually, *going back there* suddenly didn't seem like a bad idea. With his body humming and the sexual energy suddenly zapping back and forth between them, sex seemed like a good thing to consider. It wasn't, he reminded himself. It really wasn't.

''Anyway,'' she went on, after she adjusted the envelope again. ''Forget what I said. I should have kept my thoughts to myself.''

He might have had a darn good comeback for that if Rachel hadn't turned the laptop around, drawing his attention to the screen. ''There's the information you asked me to get,'' she announced.

Well, her timing was lousy. She'd basically started a verbal sparring match—about sex, no less—and he couldn't continue. Not with everything else they had to do. Besides, within the next couple of minutes, they had to leave for their meeting with Merkens.

Trying to mimic her composed exterior, but knowing they were far from composed, Jared looked at the screen. The name practically jumped out at him—and put a huge damper on the fit of temper that he wanted to nourish and feed for a while.

''Lyle Brewer,'' he read. ''Esterman's attorney?''

Rachel nodded. ''And he's one of the owners of

the company that manages the rental property for the place where Sasha Young was staying. It could be a coincidence, but I seriously doubt it.''

So did he. Anyone on Esterman's payroll was suspect. ''Maybe Brewer's the person who's been helping Esterman. Or maybe he can at least lead us in that direction.'' Jared checked his watch. ''We need to get going. I have to swap cars with Tanner before we drive to the park.''

She turned off the computer. ''You never did say—how will we recognize Aaron Merkens?''

''Easy. He said he was an Elvis impersonator. I don't think we'll have any trouble spotting him, even if he's not in costume.'' A flamboyant image popped into his head. ''God, I hope he's not in costume. I'd like to get through this without attracting an audience.''

Jared reached for his keys, only to remember another important detail. ''By the way, something else I didn't mention— Merkens demanded payment for this meeting.''

Her eyes widened. ''How much?''

''Only five hundred bucks. Don't worry, I have the money. I just thought you should know that his concern for Sasha isn't necessarily dictated by his heart. That'll tell you the kind of person we're dealing with here. In other words, I want you to be careful.''

He didn't wait for her to respond. Jared tossed her a dark blue baseball cap that he'd taken from the closet. "Here, put this on. It's a sorry excuse for a disguise, but it might buy us a little safety."

"Safety," she repeated—and paused, obviously giving that some thought. "Maybe this is a good time to ask—what exactly are you anticipating might go wrong tonight?"

Jared put his hand on the small of her back and got her moving toward the door. "Anything and everything."

Chapter Five

Jared got back in the car, bringing the scent of the rain and the park in with him. He cursed under his breath, but it wasn't so soft that Rachel couldn't hear it. Obviously, his mini reconnaissance mission hadn't gone well.

What else was new?

Not much had gone their way so far.

The cops and God knows who else were after them, and they were meeting an Elvis impersonator in a public city park. The operative word being *public*. To say she didn't have a good feeling about this was putting it mildly.

"I guess there's no sign of Merkens?" Rachel asked. She put the rest of the burger and fries that Jared had picked up for them earlier at a fast food place. It'd taken care of the hunger, but the meal hadn't made her stomach feel any better. Not that she'd expected it would. That was asking too much of mere food.

Jared shook his head and checked his watch again. "He's nearly a half hour late."

Yes. And she'd felt every single minute tick off in her head. "He might still show."

But that was wishful thinking. Rachel didn't know Aaron Merkens, but if he'd heard about the cops finding Sasha's body, then the promise of five hundred dollars might not be enough to stop him from going on the run.

And she didn't blame him.

If Jared had been able to piece together Merkens's association with Sasha, then Esterman would have been able to do the same. Esterman probably wouldn't care much for Merkens sharing information with them and might do whatever it took to stop the meeting.

In Esterman's case, *whatever it took* could mean just about anything. Including murder.

Rachel wiped the condensation off the window with a paper napkin from the sack of fast food. She had another look around. It was almost dusk, and because of the constant drizzle, the place was deserted.

Jared had parked beside some playground equipment. They were in sight and yet tucked away from the main park road—safe but definitely still out in the open. Of course, they hadn't had a choice about that. They needed Merkens to be able to see the car so he could find them.

"I should have pressed him for an earlier meeting," Jared grumbled. "Or maybe grilled him better when I got in touch with him this morning. I damn sure shouldn't have let him off the phone until I had some answers. Hell. This is costing us valuable time."

Rachel had a lot of doubts about what they were doing, but those doubts didn't include Jared's investigative skills. He'd almost certainly done his best to get whatever he could out of Merkens.

"Let's assume the worst—that he won't show. What's plan B?" she asked.

He gave her a flat look. "Believe me, there are worse things that can happen than Merkens being a no-show."

All right. She agreed with that, but it didn't help them now. They had to aim their energy in a positive direction. If there was indeed a positive one.

The phone rang, the sound cutting through the silence. "Thank God," she mumbled, hoping it was Merkens so he could explain why he wasn't there. Then, maybe Jared could browbeat him into hurrying.

Jared took the phone from his pocket and put it to his ear. "Tanner," he said several seconds later.

So she didn't get her wish, after all, but that didn't mean Merkens hadn't gotten in touch with Tanner. Unfortunately, she couldn't tell from Jared's monosyllabic responses if it was good or bad news.

Maybe Merkens had phoned to reschedule the meeting, but she prayed not. Rachel wanted to talk with him now, to get the information and then move on to the next step. Time suddenly felt like their enemy. The longer it took them to find the baby, the longer it would be before she could take the stand. Every minute was a gamble that the cops or Esterman's people would find them first.

"Tanner said he just got a call from Lyle Brewer, Esterman's attorney." Jared slipped his phone back into his pocket. "Brewer said it was important that he speak to us right away."

Lyle Brewer. Just great. First, the cops had contacted Tanner to try to get to them, and now Brewer. Maybe it wasn't a good idea for them to rely on a man who suddenly seemed too obvious a connection to them. Of course, the alternative wasn't much better. It was hard to set up security for a meeting while they were in hiding.

"Brewer says he has something important to tell us," Jared continued. "He won't say what it is until he sees us face-to-face."

Rachel's first instinct was to say no. An emphatic no. She didn't want anything to do with the man who might very well be Esterman's so-called silent partner. But the fact that Jared hadn't already vetoed the meeting meant he was at least considering it.

"You don't think Brewer would bring the baby to us, do you?" she asked. And hoped. But that would be a stupid move on his part. She knew for a fact that Esterman wasn't stupid, and doubted his attorney was, either.

"Brewer might be able to tell us more than we'll get from Merkens. If we even get anything from Merkens. I think we need all the help we can get."

Absolutely, but that information could cost them their lives. After all, Brewer owned the house where Sasha Young lived, and perhaps died.

Jared must have seen the movement at the same moment Rachel did, because his head snapped up and his gaze raced to the cluster of playground equipment near the passenger side of the car.

The man stepped around the slide and looked in their direction. He was tall. Dark hair. Wearing a tan raincoat. And he held a perky yellow umbrella over his head. Obviously, he wasn't that concerned with someone seeing him. Or maybe he simply wasn't aware of the danger.

"Stay put," Jared whispered to her as he reached for the door handle.

Staying put was certainly the safer option, but not necessarily the best one. Rachel grabbed his arm to stop him. "You're a cop through and through, Jared. I'm not. With everything that's happened, maybe Aaron Merkens will trust me more than he would you."

He didn't hesitate. Jared simply shook his head. "There's no reason for both of us to play sitting duck. Tonight, you do the sitting and I'll be the duck."

And with that decree, he must have considered the debate a done deal because he stepped out of the car and motioned for Merkens to come closer. Even that simple gesture had *cop* written all over it.

God, he was hardheaded.

Rachel held her breath and watched the encounter unfold in front of her. The two men paused as if sizing each other up, and Merkens finally started toward Jared. His long stride quickly ate up the distance between them.

Before he even reached Jared, Merkens aimed his index finger at her. "Who the hell is that? This was supposed to be a private meeting. You didn't say anything about bringing someone else along."

"Well, you didn't say anything about carrying a prissy umbrella that can be seen for miles. Trust me, that isn't a good thing. Get rid of it."

Since it seemed as if this could turn ugly, Rachel quickly stepped out of the car. Jared motioned for her to get back in, but she ignored him and extended her hand to Merkens. "Sorry to crash the meeting, but I didn't think one less duck would matter. I'm concerned about Sasha. That's why we're all here, right?"

"I guess," Merkens snarled, after apparently giving it some thought. He didn't shake her hand. Instead, he closed the umbrella and turned his attention back to Jared. "You have the money?"

"Yeah," Jared assured him. "But this is a buy now, pay later kind of deal. You give me the information about Sasha Young, and you'll get paid."

Merkens nodded, eventually, but the arrangement obviously didn't please him. He fidgeted with the plastic handle of the umbrella, and for the first time since he'd arrived, his gaze darted all around. Perhaps it was beginning to sink in that he might be in danger.

"I don't know how much more I can tell you," Merkens whispered. "Like I said, she disappeared about a week ago, and I haven't seen her since. I went by her house just this morning, but there's no sign of her. Even her clothes are gone."

He didn't know she'd been murdered. She hoped Jared wouldn't be the one to tell him. The mood among them certainly wasn't one of trust and cooperation. Hearing of Sasha's death probably wouldn't help that.

Jared kept his right hand near his shoulder holster

and weapon. "You told me on the phone that she's pregnant. Is it your baby?"

"No. Of course not." Merkens looked at him as if he'd sprouted a third eye. "It's not like that between us. She's like a sister to me. And as far as the baby, I don't know whose it is. Sasha's a surrogate for some couple who couldn't have kids. They're paying her."

"Yeah. I know that's what you said, but I wanted to make sure it's the truth." Jared's hand snaked out, and he snagged Merkens by the coat and yanked him closer. The man protested rather loudly, but that didn't stop Jared from frisking him. "Is it the truth, Aaron? Because I'd really hate to think that you're lying to me."

"According to Sasha it's true. Now, get your freakin' hands off me." He jerked away, stepped back and indignantly readjusted his coat. "I'm not carrying a gun, and I've told you all I know—so give me my money."

Keeping eye-contact with Merkens, Jared extracted a roll of bills from his jacket pocket. But he didn't hand it over. He just continued with that intimidating stare. "First, I want you to think real hard, because that's what I'm shelling out bucks for you to do. Has Sasha ever mentioned who asked her to be a surrogate?"

He immediately shook his head. "I can't help you

there. That's one thing she always stays away from. The subject of the baby is a big no-no.''

''Any theories about why she doesn't want to talk about it?'' Rachel asked.

''No. And I don't ask. I figure, it's none of my business. Like a lot of other things.'' Merkens waggled his finger at the money. ''I'll take that now.''

But Jared didn't move. ''You still have that phone number I gave you when we talked earlier? The one for a guy named Tanner?''

Merkens nodded. ''Yeah. What about it?''

''If you remember anything about who hired Sasha to be a surrogate, then call Tanner and arrange for another meeting.'' He slapped the money into Merkens's palm. ''I'll make it worth your time.''

Merkens counted the money before returning his gaze to Jared. ''I'll see what I can find out.''

''Do that, but be smart about it. No more yellow umbrellas, metaphorical or otherwise. There might be people who'd object to you digging into this.''

Merkens's eyes widened, then narrowed. He gave another nod before he turned and walked away.

''I don't think he's gotten the word yet that Sasha's dead, but he definitely knows more than he's saying,'' Jared concluded.

''How do you know that?''

''Easy. He didn't ask for an explanation when I mentioned that 'people who'd object' part. So he must at least suspect that there's more to this than me just asking a couple of questions about his friend.''

She shook her head. ''But why would Merkens withhold information? And why would he still want to meet with us if he suspected Esterman was after him?''

''He didn't keep this meeting for our benefit. He did it strictly for the money.'' Jared started back toward the car, and she followed him. ''My guess is, he needs a fix, and soon. He'll sell his soul if necessary.''

She wiped the rain off her face and slung it aside. ''So this was a waste of time?''

''Maybe. Maybe not. We've planted the seeds. When he's desperate for more money, Merkens might just recall the very piece of information that we need to know.''

Rachel was about to remind him that they might not be able to wait long enough for Merkens to come around, but a strange swishing sound stopped her. She turned her ear toward it, to try to figure out what it was, but Jared apparently already knew.

''Someone's shooting,'' he warned.

There was no time for Rachel to brace herself. No time to think.

Jared hooked his arm around her waist and pulled her to the ground. Panic gripped Rachel much faster than she could fight it off. As her heart pounded and her breath raced, the images immediately flooded her head. Her parents on the floor of their bedroom. The intruder's gun.

The smell of death.

Those images that had tormented her since she was seven years old and had witnessed their brutal murder. The memories roared through her with a vengeance.

"Try to hold it together," Jared murmured. "I'll get you out of here. I promise."

Rachel clung to the sound of his voice, clung to each comforting word. It didn't stop her physical reaction to the old demons, but she forced herself not to give in to the panic. She wouldn't let the fear cause them to get killed. Somehow, she'd get beyond this.

"The shots are coming from those trees," Jared said. He drew his own weapon. "And whoever's shooting, they're not aiming at us."

No. Not at the moment, anyway.

Rachel lifted her head a fraction and glanced at the thick oaks on the other side of the road. They were at least five hundred yards away and did a thorough job of concealing the shooter.

More shots followed. A few of them gashed into metal playground equipment and sent the creaky swing spinning. They came close. Too close. And the thought of them coming any closer sent Rachel's heart racing out of control.

She tried not to think of the baby in the photo. But her mind kept going back to that image. Unfortunately, it was spliced with the other memories racing through her head. Violent memories of her parents' murder. It was a painful reminder of the danger the child was in. Her heart ached at the thought of never learning the truth, of never seeing the baby that might be hers.

Jared levered himself up slightly and aimed his weapon. What he didn't do was fire. Thank God. She wasn't sure she could handle that with him so close to her. Instead, he paused. Waiting. Listening. Rachel listened as well, and the silence slid in around them.

Nothing.

For several excruciating moments.

Then, Rachel heard the faint sound of someone gunning a car engine. Followed by not-so-muffled gunfire.

Jared cursed. "We have company."

"Where?" Rachel looked out at the trees again but couldn't see anything.

"Two to one, the cops are here. That's why that second set of shots wasn't fired with a silencer."

Jared didn't finish the explanation. He didn't have to. If the cops were there, then they were very close to being captured.

"I doubt they want us dead," Jared continued a moment later. "But the bullets might not know that."

True. They could be killed simply because they were in the wrong place at the wrong time.

She leaped up when he did, but Jared grabbed her shoulder and pulled her right back on the ground. "Not yet."

He peered around the car door and waited for what seemed like endless minutes. By degrees, the sound of the gunfire slowly shifted in another direction. Moving away from them. Jared must have thought so as well, because he finally let her stand up, and he helped her into the car.

"We're getting out of here," he ordered. "Stay low in the seat so they can't see you."

Without turning on the headlights, Jared pulled onto the main park road and stomped on the accelerator.

"Hell," he spat out.

"What's wrong now?"

But she immediately saw what had caused Jared's reaction. When they passed a thick shrub, it was there. The body, facedown in a crumpled heap on the ground.

Rachel didn't need to see his face to know who it was. The tan trench coat. The dark hair. The yellow umbrella by his side.

It was Aaron Merkens.

And he was dead.

Chapter Six

Hell. Hell. Hell.

This was definitely a worst-case scenario coming true right before his eyes. The cops facing off against Esterman's hired assassins. This showdown could easily result in Rachel and him being captured.

Or worse.

Much, much worse.

Jared sped through the park, hoping he was moving away from both sets of shooters. He didn't have time to wait out the crossfire, and he damn sure didn't have time to stay behind and clear things up with the cops. He needed to rendezvous with Tanner in exactly a half hour, and that was one appointment he had to keep.

"They killed him," Rachel muttered under her breath. "They really killed him."

Jared added another *hell* to his mental rantings.

Rachel had obviously seen the body, and that was something he'd wanted to avoid.

''Are you all right?'' He didn't dare risk looking in her direction, but he did push her lower into the seat. Jared kept his attention on the road to make sure they weren't being followed.

She made a soft sound that couldn't hide her fear. ''I've been better.''

Yeah. A huge understatement. And the night wasn't over yet. He'd let her catch her breath first before he reminded her that this was just round one.

And they'd lost.

Merkens was dead. No doubt about that. Jared had seen the body and the blood. He didn't need a crystal ball to know who was responsible.

Clarence Esterman.

That meant Merkens had had some sensitive information that Esterman wanted to keep private. So sensitive and private that Esterman had been willing to kill to keep it secret. That also meant Jared had missed his chance to get the info—again. Hell. He should have beaten it out of the umbrella-carrying fool while he had the chance.

And while he was doling out should-have's and other insults, Jared decided he should have his own head examined for bringing Rachel into this. With her gun phobia, that shooting ordeal was probably a couple of hundred steps beyond terror. An incident like that could easily cause her to have a breakdown.

"I'll figure out a safe place for you to go as soon as I talk with Tanner," Jared promised. He made his way to an access road and then exited onto the interstate. "I won't make you go through something like this again. I swear, I'll do whatever it takes to keep you safe."

"Excuse me?"

Her tone caused him to take notice. It wasn't exactly a request for clarification. Even though her voice was trembling, it was snippy. And much too calm.

Never a good sign when it came to Rachel.

"Please don't tell me you're thinking about dumping me somewhere so you can try to find the baby all by yourself?" she asked. "You need help. *My* help. So spare me this Y-chromosome testosterone garbage."

He'd been right. Calmness in this case meant it'd take some fast talking to get Rachel to see his side. "I need you safe so I can concentrate on doing what has to be done." And to drive his point home, he added, "Do you have any idea how close you came to getting hurt tonight?"

"Some, yes. I got my first hint when that bullet whizzed past our heads and slammed into the swing just a couple of yards away."

Obviously she had a grasp on the situation. A smart-ass grasp. Jared had to unclench teeth before he could continue. "Then, you know I can't keep putting you in danger. What if you'd had a panic attack back there, huh?"

"I didn't—"

"But you could have."

"But I didn't!" She slapped her hand against the padded console. "God, I might as well find a wall to bang my head against. It'd be a better use of my time than trying to reason with you."

The sheer volume of her voice had him pausing, and it took Jared a moment to figure out why. It was the first time he ever remembered Rachel yelling at him. She wasn't the yelling type.

At least, she didn't use to be.

She obviously was now.

Rachel cursed. Not only was it loud as well, but it was also fairly creative. Had he not been the recipient of that profanity, it would have impressed him.

"Yes, I have panic attacks," she admitted, her voice still rather loud. "Yes, just the sight of a gun nearly causes me to hyperventilate. And yes, I was scared enough back there that I nearly wet my pants. But there is no way I'm going to sit on my butt and wait for you to rescue this child. Not when I can help. I'm in this as deep as you are, Jared, so learn to live with it.''

With that ultimatum, she brushed him off with one of those icy looks and folded her arms over her chest. Both things, coupled with her stubbornness, riled him.

And pleased him.

Maybe Rachel hadn't been quite as close to a panic attack as he'd originally thought. Still, that didn't mean he wanted any more bullets flying in her direction.

His brow furrowed. ''You are *so* stubborn.''

''Yeah. Like you're not?''

This was a standoff. Unlike the yelling, it was very familiar ground. He tossed a glare at her. Rachel tossed one back, and he knew she had no intention of changing her mind. So, Jared tried a more logical approach.

''What is it exactly that you believe you can do to help me find this baby faster?'' he asked. He took the exit to San Pedro Avenue where he was supposed to meet Tanner, and waited for her answer. An answer he was sure he could blast right out of the water.

''Well, for one thing, I can search hospital records on the computer to find out where Sasha had the C-section. When I have a doctor's name, we can question him and try to figure out who paid the bills.

That might lead us to the person who helped Esterman put this plan together.''

Jared had to scrutinize that response before he realized no blasting was required. As ideas went, it was a winner. It would take him hours to work his way through cyberspace, but Rachel had great hacker skills. Heck, she'd even helped him out on a few cases. She could probably figure out a way to get the information a lot faster than he could.

While he continued his mental debate about her participation, Jared parked near a bustling Mexican food restaurant. And waited.

With any luck it wouldn't take long for Tanner to show, and with even more luck, they'd be able to get lost in the crowded parking lot. Getting lost was about the safest thing they could do right now.

"Well?" she prompted. "Still thinking of a way to get rid of me?"

"It was never about me getting rid of you, Rachel. I just don't want you to have to face something that maybe you aren't ready to handle."

Rachel laughed, a short sarcastic burst of sound. "For three months I spied on Esterman. *Three months.* I suppose you think that was relaxing, huh?" She didn't wait for him to answer. She fired her words at him like gunshots. "And then he threatened to slit my throat when he heard I was going to testify. Definitely a day at the beach."

That wasn't an easy thing for him to hear. Christ! She'd done the right thing by agreeing to spy on Esterman. No one else had been in a position to bring down the man. Still, it put a knot in his gut to know that Rachel had gone through something like that.

"You know what?" she went on. "I didn't have a panic attack then, so quit treating me as if I'm a useless bimbo that you have to pawn off on someone else."

A little bewildered, he stared at her. "When did all of this happen, huh?"

"When did what happen?"

"This attitude."

"You mean me showing some backbone? It's always been there, Jared. I guess I just got out of the habit of showing it when we were together. You had enough backbone for both of us. Mine wasn't needed."

He geared up to disagree, to defend himself, but before he opened his mouth and risked inserting both of his size ten-and-a-half shoes, Jared gave it some thought. She might have a point. *Might.*

"Anyway, all of this is moot," she concluded. "We're in this together, whether you like it or not. Nod if you agree. If you don't, then please do us both a favor and keep it to yourself."

Whoa.

Jared took another mental step back to figure what

he was going to do about it. From the steely look in Rachel's eyes, her participation in this little adventure was going to happen with or without his approval. And whether he liked it or not, he really needed her help.

Only because she didn't give him a choice, Jared nodded. Eventually. "Okay. No pawning you off on anyone. But you won't take any unnecessary chances, understand?"

"Deal," Rachel practically snarled. "And I'll expect you to do the same thing. You might be six feet tall and bear a striking resemblance to a certain superhero, but you're darn sure not bullet-proof."

Flattered and rather annoyed with her sarcasm, he forced himself not to smile. Or frown. This conversation had been an eye opener.

Who *was* this woman?

He wasn't sure, but he thought he really was beginning to like her. Of course, that same backbone could cause lots of problems for them down the road.

"Minus the superhero-resemblance part, that goes for your five-and-a-half-feet tall body, as well." He added a grouchy-sounding growl for good measure.

"This might be what some would call a memorable moment. We agree on something."

"And we argued." *Really* argued. Rachel hadn't run for cover at the first sign of conflict. During their marriage, she'd been much better at freezing him out

or leaving the room than at dealing with direct confrontation.

Well, she obviously didn't have a problem with it
now.

Jared just stared at her. They were parked beneath
a neon sign, and a host of watery colors danced
across her face. The bright hues didn't quite go with
the scowl she aimed at him, but they did do some
amazing things to her eyes.

Rachel was definitely something in the looks department, and Jared had never been more aware of
that than he was at this moment. She wasn't drop-
dead gorgeous; her face was much more interesting
than gorgeous. It was an honest face. A face with
character. A few tan freckles on her nose. Great
mouth.

And suddenly she was staring as if she had no idea
what to do with him.

Unfortunately, Jared had plenty of ideas.

Bad ideas.

Something hot and intense sizzled between them.
Her scowl faded. Their gazes met, and they ex-
changed a glance that only former lovers could have
managed. A glance that conjured up the image of her
naked beneath him. And her naked on top of him.

Hell, it just conjured up sexy images, period.

"And don't you dare say that outburst was a PMS
thing," she added.

The corner of his mouth eased up, even though there sure was nothing to smile about. ''I wouldn't think of it. If I did, you might use me for a punching bag.''

The erotic images kicked up another notch. They were things he shouldn't be thinking about. Things that involved slow, wet kisses on just about every inch of her body.

The scent of her and the memory of Rachel's taste raced through him. Not good. He had too much to deal with tonight without having to fight another battle with his testosterone levels.

The timing sucked. Man, did it. She was coming down from a terrifying ordeal. For that matter, so was he. What he needed to do was step out of the car, to give her space. To give himself some space.

But Jared didn't do that.

Nope.

No space whatsoever.

Instead, he slid lower in the seat so they were eye to eye. And mouth to mouth. He eased his hand around the back of her neck and drew her closer. She didn't resist. And he didn't do a thing to encourage resistance.

She was trembling all over, and he held her, pressing his face against hers. He felt the rapid pump of her heart against his chest. Took in her rich feminine scent. Heard the slight arousing hitch of her breath that told him surrender of some sort was just around the corner. If he wanted her to surrender, that is.

He assured himself that he didn't.

He really didn't.

But even that assurance didn't stop the slow hunger that made its way through him. And he knew he was in trouble. Still, he didn't do a thing to stop it. In fact, he sped things along.

Cursing himself, Jared did something he figured he'd soon regret. He leaned in, gathered her close and captured Rachel's mouth as if it were his for the taking.

Chapter Seven

It was instantaneous. Rachel heard the crash of thunder outside. Inside, there was a flash of heat between Jared and her.

He pulled her to him, his arms warm and welcome. The motion was seamless and surprisingly gentle. However, that was the only thing happening between them that was gentle. His mouth was suddenly on her.

That clever, hot mouth.

Maybe it was from bone-weary fatigue or just the fire that had always been there, but Rachel felt her willpower dissolve the moment he kissed her. Every wall that she'd built to distance herself from him came tumbling down.

He looked good. Smelled good. But, sweet mercy, he tasted even better.

He plunged her into a fire so hot that it nearly consumed her on the spot. The mating of their tongues. The intimate joining of their mouths. The heat of their bodies. The way they fit together, even now.

Jared was good. Beyond good. But then, she'd always known that. He could somehow turn a simple kiss into something almost as good as full-blown sex.

Almost.

Her body quickly reminded her that it was *almost* as good.

His tongue teased hers. His mouth pleasured. And it left her wanting more in the worst kind of way. A way Rachel knew she couldn't have.

Not now, at least.

After all, they were in a parking lot. Out in the open. Where anyone could see them.

Or kill them.

Jared's awareness of their situation must have kicked in at the exact moment as hers, because Rachel felt his sinewy arms tense just slightly. At first. Then, they tensed a lot more than slightly.

His mouth left hers, and he eased back a couple of inches. His breathing was uneven. His lips slightly parted. Their gazes came together again, and this time the heat was mixed with a fair amount of reality.

Reality wasn't especially welcome, since she still had the taste of him in her mouth.

"Guess that was one of those act now, think later kind of reactions," he mumbled.

"Yes."

There wasn't much else she could say. Without him feeding the fire in her blood, the kiss seemed, well, incredibly stupid. Here they were in the middle of a dangerous situation, having just witnessed a murder, and they couldn't keep their hormones in check.

Yes, definitely stupid.

"I was way out of line," he added. "And I'm sorry."

"Yeah. Me too."

But it was a lie. Rachel wasn't sorry that he'd kissed her; she was sorry that it had felt so good.

She wanted to try to explain away the whole incident, but she changed her mind when she heard the sound of an approaching vehicle. A sporty black truck. It drove past them. Slowly. The driver didn't park in the front of the main lot where they were but instead drove to the back.

The far back.

It was still within sight but barely. Rachel could see the vehicle in her side mirror.

"That's Tanner," Jared said. "And I'll bet Lyle Brewer won't be too far behind him. Make sure you stay low in the seat. The windows are tinted, but I don't want to take any chances."

What was left of that ember of passion evaporated

on the spot. "Brewer, as in Esterman's attorney? What would he be doing here?"

"Meeting with Tanner. Remember, Brewer says he has something he needs to tell us."

Her mouth dropped open. Jared had already agreed to the meeting—and set it up—without even getting her opinion? So that's what the monosyllabic conversation with Tanner had been about.

"I thought I made it clear that I didn't want to be left out of the information loop," Rachel insisted.

"You won't be left out. Tanner stashed this in the car for us." Jared picked up a small receptor earpiece and ink-pen size communicator from the tray beneath the console. "We'll be able to hear everything Brewer says."

"That's not what I meant, and you know it. I should be the one to meet with Brewer. Esterman wants me alive. He probably doesn't feel the same about Tanner. Or you."

"Brewer doesn't know you're here, all right." Jared made use of the receptor, holding it against his ear. "He thinks you're someplace miles away, and I want to keep it that way."

So did she, but not at the risk of endangering someone else. Still, there was little she could do about it now. Jared had already set things into motion.

Tanner got out of his vehicle, the wind and the

drizzle spitting at him. Rachel recognized him immediately. Hard not to remember the desperado-dark hair that stopped just at the top of his shoulders. He always reminded her of a vampire who'd turned good but had a fifty-fifty chance of going back to his old biting ways. Still, Jared trusted him, so that had to count for something.

Just how much of something, Rachel didn't yet know.

After all, Tanner had obviously agreed with Jared to set up this meeting. She'd reserve judgment on whether that was a good thing.

Rachel leaned closer so she could share the receptor with Jared. He held it between them, but since the device was so small, she had to get closer. Very close. Until they were shoulder to shoulder and practically cheek to cheek.

Great.

The closeness wasn't an ideal arrangement so soon after they'd shared that kiss. But then, there was nothing about this situation that was ideal.

"Jared, Rachel," Tanner greeted, obviously speaking into some hidden communicator. He leaned against his truck and waited.

"Was this get-together your idea?" Rachel asked Tanner. Unfortunately, she had to lean against Jared to ask that. Her left breast pressed against his arm.

Jared noticed. He grunted softly. So did she.

Unaware of the touchy-feely session going on in the car, Tanner shrugged. "It was sort of a mutual decision. I think it's possible that Lyle Brewer knows a lot more about what's going on than he'll want to share with Jared or you."

She glanced at Jared. "I didn't need a meeting to tell me that. Has it occurred to you two that this might not be safe? A man was just killed, for heaven's sake. Brewer could be leading the gunmen or the cops right to us."

"Not tonight he's not," Tanner assured her. "We left the gunmen in the park." He pulled out a small bag of something from his pocket and started eating. Peanuts, she realized when she saw him throw the shells onto the ground. The man was certainly calm under pressure. Unlike her.

Rachel huffed. "And you think they'll just stay there because that's where you left them?"

"They'll need to clear up that mess they made with umbrella-boy. They won't want that kind of evidence left lying around for the cops to find." Tanner took his time munching on another peanut. "Plus, I arranged a little diversion for them when they're done with that. Esterman's men think you're at a hotel on the west side of town. They're likely providing that information to the cops as we speak."

That wasn't much of a reassurance. Diversions weren't necessarily a success just because they were diversions. Still, it was too late to do anything about it. They were here, ready to meet with Lyle Brewer. It was best to learn what they could from him, and then get the heck out of here.

Tanner tipped his head toward the front of the parking lot. "Speaking of the devil, there's Brewer. I do so admire a person who's on time for their appointments."

A sleek midnight-black car drove in and came to a stop just a couple of yards behind Tanner's truck.

"Stay down, Rachel," Jared warned.

From the side mirror she could see Lyle Brewer exit his car. She had no trouble recognizing him, as well. The perfectly styled salt-and-pepper hair. The polished demeanor. She'd seen him in Esterman's office numerous times. He was no doubt doing everything possible to get his client out of jail. Was he also in on the plan to hold a child hostage in exchange for her false testimony?

Rachel could certainly believe that. After all, Brewer worked for Esterman.

"For the sake of your suit, we'd better make this quick," Tanner insisted when he greeted Brewer. "I've heard overpriced Italian suits shrink when they get wet."

That didn't do a lot to improve Brewer's demeanor. Even at a distance, Rachel could see his shoulders stiffen.

"I spoke with my client's personal assistant this afternoon, and he asked me to get a message to Lieutenant Dillard."

"Oh, yeah?" Tanner tossed down another peanut shell. It landed on or near Brewer's shoes. "Does your client's personal assistant have a name?"

"He wishes to remain in the shadows, so to speak, but he assures me that he's acting on behalf of Mr. Esterman himself. Mr. Esterman is weary of the court proceedings and the trial delays, and he believes he'll be exonerated when the jury has all the evidence. So, he humbly requests that Rachel Dillard turn herself over to the proper authorities so she can testify."

"And if she doesn't?" Tanner challenged.

Brewer shrugged. "I'm not here to issue warnings or threats. I simply want a fair trial for my client."

Tanner chuckled. "In a pig's eye. You want him to walk."

Brewer nodded without hesitation. "That, too. No surprise there—he is, after all, my client. But I'm of no threat to the lieutenant or Rachel Dillard. I'm simply asking them to comply with the law. That shouldn't be a far stretch for the lieutenant, since he's a peace officer. I've heard rumblings that in a matter of hours, the chief of police will be demanding Dillard's badge."

Even though Jared didn't move or make a sound, Rachel was close enough to feel him tense. That was it. His only reaction to what had to be heartbreaking news. It was another of those weird ironies. Jared had done the right thing by stopping her testimony, but in doing so, he'd broken the law.

"Are you okay?" she whispered.

"Sure."

It was a lie. And even more than that, it was a taboo subject. During their marriage, they'd disagreed so many times over his devotion to his badge that just bringing it up now would make things worse.

Rachel turned her attention back to Brewer just as he slipped his hand into his jacket.

Before she could even blink, Tanner dropped the bag of peanuts, reached into his jacket and drew his weapon. So did Jared. He didn't stop there. He opened the car door a fraction.

With her heart pounding, she held her breath and waited. God, she'd known this could turn dangerous but she hadn't expected it to happen so quickly. If Jared was forced to fire to protect Tanner and if Esterman's people waited nearby, it would almost certainly lead to another gun battle.

"I'm not armed," Brewer assured him, his voice shaking now. "I just need to retrieve some correspondence from my pocket."

"No sudden moves, and use only two fingers," Tanner instructed.

Keeping his gaze locked with that of the man who had a gun aimed at him, Brewer extracted the envelope and stiffly extended it to Tanner. "From Mr. Esterman's personal assistant."

Tanner took it. What he didn't do was lower his weapon. "I'd love to do this the old-fashioned way and coax the information out of you, but I don't have time. So here goes— Where's the baby?"

Rachel moved to the edge of the seat and wished the rain and the darkness weren't between them so she could better see Brewer's expression. It was a long shot, but she might be able to figure out just how deep he was into this.

"I have no idea what you're talking about," Brewer insisted. "What baby?"

Tanner stood there for several moments, studying him. "Why don't you ask your boss? And while you're asking, tell him that he can contact me with the answer."

"I will. Not that I expect him to know, either. By the way, I'd like to offer some free advice. Personally, I'm not as anxious as my client to see Rachel Dillard on the stand, but it's my duty to advise you or her husband to take her to the nearest police station."

No long pause this time. Tanner's response was immediate. "Here's some free advice right back at you—go to hell and take your scumbag client with you.''

If Brewer had a reaction to that, he didn't show it. He simply turned and walked back to his car.

Tanner waited until Brewer had driven away before he got back in his truck. Rachel could hear him opening the envelope.

''Well?'' Jared asked. ''What was so hell-fired important that Esterman had to tell us?''

''It's a blank page,'' Tanner relayed to them.

Rachel shook her head. ''What does that mean?''

Jared started the car. ''It means Esterman's people will be following Tanner so they can try to find us.''

Of course they would. That's the reason they'd wanted this meeting in the first place. ''And what will we be doing?''

''Following Brewer.'' He pulled out of the parking lot and onto the street. The car was just ahead, in the flow of traffic. ''It's time we found out just how much he really knows about the baby.''

Chapter Eight

"Well?" Rachel asked the moment Jared ended the call with the fertility clinic. She stared at him, tension showing all over her face. "What did they say?"

Not what Jared had wanted them to say, that was for sure.

He handed Rachel the cell phone so she could reconnect it to the modem for the laptop. "Both the fertilized embryos and unfertilized eggs were stolen."

"Great." She blew out a ragged breath. "So the baby…"

"Could be yours or ours," he supplied when she didn't finish.

"Or neither."

"Yeah. But then, we've known that was a possibility right from the start." Despite the seriousness of the conversation, Jared kept a close watch on Lyle Brewer's vehicle that was two cars ahead of him.

"So, where does that leave us?" Rachel asked.

"Not where I'd like us to be, but there's some good news. Well, potentially good news, anyway. Whoever stole the embryos left two unfertilized eggs, so the hospital can get a sample of your DNA from those and match it to the saliva swab that was in the envelope. They'll soon be able to figure out if the child is yours."

She obviously followed that to the next logical step. "And what about *your* DNA?"

"I donated blood just a couple of weeks ago, and thankfully the hospital still had it. We could know something as early as tomorrow morning."

She didn't say a word, but Jared knew what she was thinking. Tomorrow morning might be too late. It was anybody's guess as to when the cops or Esterman's men would find them and haul them in.

He finished off the rest of his cold cheeseburger and continued to follow Lyle Brewer. After they'd left the parking lot at the Mexican food restaurant, Brewer had dropped off his dry cleaning, used the ATM at the bank and picked up a prescription at a drive-through all-night pharmacy. In other words, routine stuff. He certainly didn't seem to be a man on the verge of revealing the location of the baby.

Rachel's fingers stilled on the computer keyboard for a few seconds when Brewer turned down another street. "He lives somewhere in this area. You think he's going home now?"

"I sure hope not."

But what Jared hoped for was a long shot. He wanted Brewer to lead them straight to the child. Tonight.

Talk about a tall order.

It was entirely possible that Brewer had no part in any of this, but Jared had to make sure. Besides, now that Aaron Merkens was dead, Brewer was one of the few leads they had. God help them.

They followed the car for another mile before Brewer stopped for gas. Jared waited on the narrow side street next to the store and hoped that the attorney hadn't caught on to the fact that he'd been tailed for the better part of an hour. If so, then God knows how long Brewer would keep driving around in the hopes of losing them. Or boring them to death.

"I don't guess you've found anything in those hospital files?" Jared asked, glancing at the computer screen.

"No. But that could be important information in itself. If there's no hospital record, that means Esterman's people probably used a private facility to do the C-section. But even private facilities can leave paper trails."

Yeah. But it was another long shot. What they needed was a break—and soon.

Because it was too heart-wrenching to consider, Jared hadn't let himself dwell on the possibility that Esterman might not even keep the baby alive. According to the evidence Rachel had unearthed during her undercover surveillance, Esterman had killed before.

Plenty of times.

Jared pushed that to the back of his mind. If he started dealing in what-if's when it came to the baby's fate, he wouldn't be able to do his job. And he couldn't let that happen.

He eased back out into traffic to follow Brewer from the gas station. The rain kept up a slow steady drizzle. The wipers slashed across the windshield and blended with the sound of Rachel's keystrokes on the computer. He heard her breathe and make that odd little sound she made when she was frustrated.

"Despite our differences about my Neanderthal approach to conflict resolution, I'm glad we're doing this together," he said.

Her fingers stilled. What she didn't do was look at him.

"Me, too."

The moment was oddly right, despite everything that was oddly wrong. He might have said more. He might even have apologized for everything that had gone on between them, but the moment was over when Jared had to make the next turn to follow Brewer.

Brewer drove into an upscale residential area, went several blocks and came to a stop in front of a large colonial-style home. Jared killed the headlights and stayed back, parking behind another car just up the street.

"The address is 623 Hanshaw Lane," Rachel provided. She grabbed her notes from the console and scanned them. "It's not Brewer's place, but he lives a few miles from here."

Jared craned his neck to get a better view of the front of the house. "There's no name on the mailbox. Think you can find out whose place this is?"

"Hopefully."

She got to work, her fingers dancing over the keyboard. Jared kept his attention on Brewer. With his briefcase clutched in his hand, the attorney exited his car and walked up the sidewalk to the front door. Jared barely got a glimpse of the man who answered.

White male. About six feet tall. Silver-gray hair.

"Got it. It's the residence of Donald Livingston." Rachel's gaze raced across the screen before her eyes widened. She turned to him. "He's the warden, Jared. The warden of the prison where Sasha Young was incarcerated."

"Bingo." And despite the fact that it still was a long shot, Jared smiled.

"Wait. I'm positive I recognize that name. Let me check something." Rachel typed in another search. "Yes, I was right. He's Clarence Esterman's former client."

Okay. Jared hadn't expected that, but it might fit nicely. "In what capacity?"

She entered more information, but shook her head when she got the results. "I don't know. Livingston's name is listed in the company's records, but it appears his files were among those that Esterman deleted."

"Even better. Esterman wouldn't have deleted them unless there was a reason. I think we just might have gotten our first big break."

"Yes." Rachel pulled in a long breath. "But what do we do with it?"

His smile faded. Good question. He had answers, but Jared wasn't sure how they fit with the questions.

"Keep digging for information on Warden Livingston," Jared told her. "It's too risky for us to sit here all night, but I'll have Tanner assign one of his detectives to watch the house. When the place is empty, we'll go inside and have a look around."

"Breaking and entering?" she asked.

Her tone was just slightly too self-satisfied for his liking. "You got a better idea?"

"No. I'm willing to do whatever it takes."

Good. Because it would take a lot. Jared was absolutely sure of that.

"YOU'RE SUPPOSED TO BE resting," Jared pointed out, glancing at her over his shoulder.

"So are you," Rachel countered.

She closed her eyes for a few seconds, but when she opened them, the words on the computer screen were still just as blurry as they had been for the past hour.

Cursing the fatigue, Rachel set the laptop aside, got up from the bed and went into the bathroom to splash some water on her face. Her head was pounding. Her mouth was like a wad of cotton. And every muscle in her body was knotted to the point of being painful.

Sometime in the four hours since she and Jared had checked into the low-budget hotel, the surge of adrenaline had caused her to crash and burn, leaving her with a bone-weary fatigue that a hot shower definitely hadn't cured. What she needed was a good night's sleep. Which she wouldn't get anytime soon.

She checked her clothes that she'd hung over the towel rack after her shower. Still too damp to put back on. The bed-sheet toga would have to do a while longer. Not good. Even though she was covered from shoulder to toes, it seemed a little risqué to walk around wearing just a sheet with her soon-to-be-ex in the room. And it wasn't her imagination that Jared had noticed the sheet, either.

He'd definitely noticed.

And *she'd* noticed that *he'd* noticed.

The attraction was still there between them, just as it had been from the first day Rachel had seen him waiting on the steps of the campus administration building.... It was winter. Her senior year in college. He stood there, an icy breeze stirring his long black coat. And his hair. When she caught his gaze, he smiled, causing a dimple to flash in his cheek. She was already half in love with him before she learned that he was a cop.

Odd that the physical attraction would survive and the love wouldn't.

"Are you okay?" Jared called out.

"Just taking a little break."

And going through her own version of hormone Hades. The adrenaline might have caused a crash and burn, but it didn't do a thing to dull her senses. At the moment, a good sense-dulling would have been a blessing.

Gathering up her toga so she wouldn't trip, Rachel walked back through the room and peeked out the window. The cars trickled past on the nearby high-way, but on the other side of the six lanes, she could see the street that led to Livingston's neighborhood.

They were still five miles away but could easily be there in less than ten minutes.

But first they had to get the go-ahead from Tanner.

It was approaching midnight, and they still hadn't received a call from the investigator that Tanner had placed near Livingston's house. Not that she'd expected that call before morning. However, Rachel had prayed that Livingston would leave so they could figure out if he had any information to link him to the baby.

Livingston was divorced, she'd learned from her computer search. No kids. And he lived alone. What Rachel couldn't be certain of was that he was truly *alone*. There could be someone else staying in the house. A lover. A relative. A housekeeper. Any one of them could pose a problem when she and Jared actually went inside the house. Still, it was their best bet for finding new information.

At the moment, their only bet.

She hadn't wanted to let herself hope, but were Esterman's people holding the baby there? It didn't seem logical that a man of Donald Livingston's reputation would risk something like that, but the child had to be somewhere. Besides, Livingston was one of the few connections they had to Sasha Young. Livingston and Lyle Brewer.

And in a bizarre circle, both of them were connected to Esterman.

"You should try to get some sleep," Jared reminded her. "God knows, you need it."

She made a sound of agreement. "This coming from a man who's put in more hours than I have. How long have you had that envelope, anyway?"

He didn't answer right away, which meant he knew where her comment was leading. "Since around eleven o'clock last night. A courier brought it to the town house."

"So that means you've been working twenty-four hours straight, but my guess is it's been even longer than that since you've had any sleep."

"You'd guess right." He looked at her over his shoulder. There was nothing especially incredible about that look except the fact that Jared was the one doing the looking.

From the moment he'd told her about the baby, Rachel had tried to prepare herself for all the challenges she might face. However, the challenge at the moment was all the feelings for him that still whispered inside her. Those whispers were rapidly turning into a roar.

Keeping her hands plastered to her side so she wouldn't be tempted to touch him, she walked closer. From over his shoulder she saw that he'd spread out the contents of the envelope on the desk. The letter, the DNA results and the two photographs. Jared was reading the letter, probably to see if there were any hidden clues. And as with her computer search for hospital records, it didn't appear that he'd been successful in finding anything else. Still, he was plugging away at it.

Devoted to duty. That was Jared, all right. Always on the job. But this time, he didn't have the support of his fellow officers and he couldn't use his badge. Despite all that, he hadn't given up. And that brought Rachel back to something she'd been mulling over all afternoon.

"I've decided to call your captain," she informed him. "I'll tell her that it was my decision to leave the safe house, that I forced you to come with me. It might get you out of hot water."

He turned around in the chair to face her. "Thanks for the offer, but I knew the consequences before I went to see you this morning."

"I know. And that probably made it a thousand times harder for you." She paused, keeping her gaze on the computer screen. "I'll make that call after we learn what we can from Livingston."

"No, you won't. I'd rather you focus on finding the paper trail for the medical facility that did Sasha Young's C-section. I'll settle up with the captain when this is over."

"But then it might be too late to save your badge."

He flexed his eyebrows and turned his attention

back to the letter. "Are you having trouble figuring out if that's a good or a bad thing?"

A year ago, that would have sent her into one heck of sulking session, but Rachel was too tired to sulk. Besides, it was an honest question.

"I never wanted you to lose your badge, Jared."

"No?" He shrugged. "You just wanted me to give it up voluntarily."

That was the truth. But only because he'd come so close to dying. Still, that admission was another sulking session in the making. In Jared's opinion, possible death was part of the job description.

"I don't want to go through this tonight." She rubbed her hand over her face. "Those old issues don't even matter anymore. We're practically divorced, and the only thing really left between us is to find this baby."

It wasn't exactly true. If they found the baby, there would certainly be tons of other issues to work out, but they seemed miles away.

"What about the lust you mentioned earlier?" he asked. Not calmly, either. There was an edge to his question. "That's certainly still between us. If you're keeping a tally, it has to go somewhere at the top of the list."

She had to hand it to him—Jared knew how to keep her on her toes. Or maybe that was designed to knock her off her toes a bit since they were breaching taboo waters. Rachel hoped her body didn't get any ideas from all this lust talk.

It wasn't an invitation.

"Okay, we'll put lust as number two on the list, right after finding the baby," Rachel said, and she took up where he left off. "And for three, we can add all this knight-to-the-rescue stuff that you dole out. That's still between us, as well. Even now."

"I beg your pardon?"

She leaned her hip against the table. "I've had a lot of time to think over the past year, and I believe you married me because you have a knight complex. It's a dominant part of your personality."

"You mean because I took care of my mom and kid sister after my dad ran out on us?"

Rachel nodded. "And you did that when most teenagers couldn't have handled it." She smiled when he scowled. "Don't look insulted—it was an honorable and selfless thing to do. You continued that selfless lifestyle by becoming a cop. Then I arrived on the scene, and, well, let's just say I was the ultimate damsel in distress to keep fueling all your knightly impulses."

"Because you have panic attacks." He spared her a considering glance. "And you believe these selfless knightly impulses of mine were the reason we got together?"

She didn't really care for the way he phrased that. "That was a large part of it, yes."

"You left out the lust again."

Great. He just wouldn't get off that subject, and it wasn't a safe one for them to dwell on. "I meant to leave it out. Because despite its prominent place on this theoretical list, it no longer applies to us—even if it feels like it does. It's a facade, an illusion, brought on by adrenaline, forced proximity...and this blasted toga."

He smiled, but like his comments, there was something a little off about it. Something hot and dangerous simmering just below the surface.

It sure felt like an invitation.

To something.

Rachel pushed herself away from the table and started to pace. Jared just sat there. Staring. "What, no opinions about that?" she asked.

"You tell me what I think," Jared challenged. This time she got more than a glance. And it was more than a considering one. He stood and raked his gaze over her.

Oh boy. The man certainly knew how to put some spin on a simple gaze.

"It doesn't matter now, anyway." She tried to sound dispassionate. And failed miserably.

"Wrong guess. That wasn't what I was thinking."

She scowled at his sarcasm. Or, at least, she tried

to scowl. Since that wasn't working, it seemed a really good time for that nap, so Rachel turned to head for the bed.

Jared obviously had other ideas.

He snagged her wrist so fast that she didn't even see it coming. But then he stopped. Stared at her. And eased his grip slightly as if to give her the chance to retreat. When she didn't, when she met that challenging stare of his without backing down, he drew her closer and pressed her hand right against the front of his jeans.

He was aroused.

Mercy.

Fully aroused.

And so was she.

"I don't want you to do anything about this, got it?" he grumbled. "I just want you to know that our marriage might have failed, but the attraction didn't. So that lust part definitely still applies, without any qualifiers. Got it?"

Rachel expected to see some sort of battle going on in his golden-brown eyes. But there was no battle. No hesitation. And that sent a wild rush through her.

He moved his hand away.

She needed to do something, to say something to make this situation better. But nothing good came to mind. Unfortunately, something bad did.

She didn't move her hand.

"Rachel," he warned.

"You put it there." She'd meant to make it sound arrogant, but there was nothing arrogant about her tone, her touch. Or especially her mood.

And Jared reacted.

He leaned in, slowly, and touched his mouth to hers. She'd braced herself for a full assault like the one in the car, but this was an assault of a different kind. Just as potent. Just as arousing. Just as lethal. Her body suddenly felt as if it were about to burn from the inside out.

"We used to be good at this," he reminded her, his mouth moving like silk over hers.

It took her a moment to find her breath. "We apparently still are."

With that affirmation, he went back for seconds. His mouth was warm. Possessive. Thorough. And welcome. He went lower, nipping her bottom lip with his teeth. He went lower still and used that clever mouth on her throat. On her pulse. On that much-too-sensitive spot just below her ear.

Without stopping the kiss, he released his grip and slid his fingers along her arm. To her breast. He eased down the makeshift toga. A fraction.

But it was just enough.

She whimpered when his lips pressed against the swell of her right breast. She cried out when he circled her nipple with his tongue. By the time he had taken her into his mouth, Rachel had all but collapsed against him.

She begged for mercy.

She begged for more.

He gave her both.

Jared gave her other breast the same attention. The same tongue kiss. The same fire bath. Then, he repositioned the sheet to cover her and eased away. Not easily. And only after a couple of hard breaths and a throat clearing. But he eventually eased away from her.

"Nice toga," he managed to say. Again, not easily. But he finally got out the words. "Now, wasn't that more relaxing than pacing the floor or straightening a stack of magazines?"

She couldn't answer right away. "I'd say so."

"Liar."

The corner of his mouth eased up ever so slightly, but he didn't put that lethal, sexy grin to work—something that would have caused her to push things just to see how far they would go. Instead, he helped her into bed and tucked her in.

"Sleep tight, Rachel."

Not a chance. Not with her worries about the baby, Esterman and Livingston. Not with this renewed attraction she felt for Jared.

No, a restful night's sleep probably wasn't in the cards for her tonight. Still, Rachel snuggled deep into the covers and closed her eyes.

Chapter Nine

All they had to do was literally walk in the place. No one was home because Donald Livingston had already left for work. Tanner's people had deactivated the security system, unlocked the doors, and had even done an infrared scan to make sure the house was empty.

It was.

So why didn't all those precautions make Jared feel even marginally better?

He stood behind a row of stately white pillars on the back porch, his hand on the door and Rachel by his side. He contemplated the uneasy feeling that had settled in his stomach. Maybe it was from lack of sleep, even though both Rachel and he had managed to get a couple of hours of much-needed rest. Maybe the uneasiness was simply because they were at the residence of the man who might have the child. Or maybe it was nothing at all.

"Is something wrong?" Rachel whispered.

Highly probable, but that wasn't what he said to her. "Everything's fine." And while Jared was doling out assurances, he tried to convince himself—again—that they were doing the right thing.

He wished that Rachel weren't with him for this one, but the alternative was leaving her in the hotel room with Tanner. That might help lessen the uneasy feeling, but it'd rile the hell out of her. With reason. She had as much right to do this as he did.

Even if it went against his gut feeling.

His instincts were to protect her, especially now, to shield her from the things that might hurt her. But Jared was quickly learning that Rachel no longer wanted that from him. It was possible she never had. Maybe it was something he'd assumed she wanted—and needed.

He was quickly learning that he'd been wrong about a lot of things when it came to her.

"Is this a good time to remind you to focus on what we're supposed to be doing?" Rachel grumbled, obviously impatient that they were still lurking around outside Livingston's house. "The sun's starting to rise, and I'd rather not wait out here much longer."

Jared pushed her impatience aside and listened one last time for something he didn't hear. No footsteps.

No whispered sounds. No indication whatsoever that there was anyone else on the property.

Hoping the uneasy feeling was just a fluke, but not totally dismissing it, either, Jared opened the door and got them inside.

''I need to find Livingston's computer,'' Rachel reminded him.

He certainly hadn't forgotten that. It was the main reason they were here. If the warden had left any incriminating evidence, the computer was their best bet. But now, to find it. The house was sprawling, and it would take hours just to search the place.

Making their way through the kitchen, they meandered through a series of rooms before they located an office. Rachel didn't waste any time. She sat at the desk and got to work while Jared had a look around.

Nothing seemed out of the ordinary. The room was utilitarian with coffee-colored paneling and lots of filled bookshelves. There were plaques and framed awards neatly arranged on the mantel above a stone fireplace. One award from the mayor. Another, from the chief of police. From all appearances, Livingston was a model citizen.

But something about it didn't ring right.

He was almost *too* model.

There were two doors leading off the room. One led to a covered patio area and beyond that was a swimming pool. Jared eased open the other door to Livingston's bedroom. Like the rest of the house, it was large. And perfect. The four-poster bed was made with precision. The matching throw rugs were straight. No scattered clothing. The only sign that it wasn't a static display was the glass of water on the nightstand next to the bed.

Livingston was obviously a perfectionist. Not good. Attention to detail wasn't an asset that Jared wanted in a suspect. He'd take a sloppy opportunist any day.

"Stay put," he told Rachel. "I'll look around in the bedroom."

"Wait, I might have found something already."

Jared quickly crossed the room to the oversize desk. Rachel was searching through the "Sent Items" folder in Livingston's e-mail inbox.

"Livingston has his defaults set so that his computer automatically saves a copy of each message that he sends out. It's a break for us and an even bigger break that he hasn't deleted them."

She pointed out a pair of messages sent to a Dr. Randall Sheridan. But it wasn't just the word *Doctor* that garnered Jared's attention. It was the dates. Livingston had sent the messages exactly one week ago.

The date the baby was probably born.

Rachel opened the first message. It was short and sweet. "'Inform me when procedure is complete and the outcome,'" she read aloud. She clicked onto the next one. "'Payment for your services will arrive by courier.'"

"Payment," Jared repeated.

He glanced at the time difference between the messages. A little over two hours. That was most likely enough time for Dr. Sheridan to have completed the C-section and given Livingston the news. Of course, it was entirely possible that this message thread had nothing to do with Sasha Young or the baby.

But Jared's gut instincts said otherwise.

"Go ahead and have a look around the rest of the house," Rachel insisted. "I'll see if I can retrieve the messages that the doctor sent to Livingston."

It was a good idea, but Jared didn't intend to get too far away from Rachel. He left her to do her e-mail search and went back into the adjoining bedroom. If Livingston had left what might be critical information on his computer, he might have left it elsewhere, too.

Jared checked the drawer of the nightstand, but it was empty except for some generic-brand condoms. Even though he tried to stave off the thoughts, the condoms reminded him of sex.

And Rachel.

But, of course, he hadn't really needed the condoms to ignite any memories or lustful thoughts. In the past twenty-four hours, despite fatigue, danger and the harrowing search for the child, he'd thought about sex a lot.

And Rachel.

Once this was behind them, he really needed to sit down and figure out what they were going to do about, well, everything. Whatever they'd thought was over between them had certainly gotten a second wind. It had for him, anyway, and he was almost certain Rachel felt the same. Especially after that toga incident. But the real issue was—would either of them be willing to take the kind of risk necessary to jump into another relationship?

Again, he relied on his gut feeling. After those toga kisses, just about anything was possible.

Forcing his attention back to his search, Jared glanced into the small, color-coordinated trash can that was near the massive walk-in closet.

Nothing.

The closet itself didn't look promising either. Shoes, clothes and ties in such perfect arrangement that it made Jared shake his head. Still, he rifled through the shelves to make sure nothing had been tucked out of sight.

He had just pulled aside a stack of crisp white undershirts when he heard the sound.

A *click*.

Just a click.

And then Jared's worst fears came true. Because the *click* was the sound of a door opening.

Not in the bedroom.

But in the office where Rachel was still working on the computer.

Drawing his weapon, Jared quietly rushed to the door and peered into the bedroom. Empty. He hurried to the entrance to the office, and the second he made it there, the lights in that particular room flared on. He caught just a glimpse of the snow-haired man coming in through the patio.

Donald Livingston had apparently come home.

Hell.

"I just have to change my clothes," he said to someone. "I won't be long."

Silently cursing himself and their rotten luck, Jared frantically glanced around the office and finally spotted Rachel beneath the desk. She looked terrified but was unharmed. Thank God.

From Livingston's angle, he wouldn't be able to see her. Well, hopefully not. But that might not last. Besides, Jared knew *he* was in a highly visible spot if Livingston came into the bedroom.

Jared debated just latching onto Livingston and holding him at gunpoint so Rachel could escape, but he had no idea who was on the other side of that patio door. If it was a hired thug, Rachel would be in more danger than she was now.

He motioned for Rachel to stay quiet, and then scrambled beneath the bed so he could still see the corner of the desk in the office. God knows how long it would take the man to change his clothes, but Jared hoped Livingston would do it immediately and get the devil out of there.

Livingston strolled into the bedroom, his pricey leather shoes whispering over the thick platinum-colored rug. And then—damn it—he shut the door.

Jared choked back a wave of fear and concentrated on listening for Rachel. If the other visitor came into the office and spotted her, Jared would almost certainly hear her react. And then he'd get to her, no matter what that took.

Even if it meant going through Livingston first.

Jared pulled in his breath, kept his gun ready and braced himself for whatever was about to happen.

OH GOD.

She'd barely made it under the desk in time. Another second, and Livingston would have seen her at his computer. She prayed he wouldn't look in the direction of the monitor, because he would notice that it had been turned on.

This was obviously one of those worst-case scenarios that Jared was always talking about. At least, that's what Rachel thought when Livingston slipped into his bedroom and shut the door.

She was so wrong.

The worst was yet to come.

Almost immediately she heard another sound. The rattle of a doorknob a split second before it opened, and it wasn't the one from the bedroom where Livingston had just entered. It was the one that led from the patio, and that sound sent Rachel's heart to her throat.

Someone strolled into the office. She'd known Livingston was talking to someone outside, but Rachel had prayed the other person wouldn't come in. But not only was this person in the house, but the sound of footsteps seemed to be coming straight for the desk.

Rachel squeezed herself as far back as she could go. Drawing her knees against her chest, she tried not to make a sound. She tried not to breathe, hoping Jared would stay put, as well. She didn't even want to speculate about what would happen if he came bursting out of that bedroom with a gun in his hand.

The footsteps stopped. Directly in front of her. And she saw the visitor's legs. It was a man wearing dress slacks, and he was so close she could have reached out and touched him.

She pressed her fingertips to her mouth. And waited. She didn't have to wait long. He moved quickly. Away from the front of the desk. Behind it.

Behind her.

"Mind telling me what you're doing down there?" the man snarled.

The sound that she'd choked back escaped as a small, barely audible gasp. A thousand thoughts went through her head. None good. But she forced herself not to panic. Maybe she could defuse this situation so Jared wouldn't have to use his gun.

Praying, Rachel crawled out from beneath the desk and looked up at him. Whoever he was, he was huge and towered over her. A wide face, hulking shoulders, and a thick head of cropped blond curls.

However, it wasn't just his physical appearance that sent her heart pounding. It was the shoulder holster and gun she saw beneath his open jacket. That coupled with his mere presence would have been enough to scare her, but it was only the beginning. Her gaze landed on his name tag.

Sergeant Colby Meredith.

This was the very person that Jared suspected of being a leak in the department, and he was also likely on Esterman's payroll.

Now, *this* was a worst-case scenario.

Rachel somehow got to her feet. How, she didn't know. Her whole body suddenly felt as sturdy as cotton balls, and there was a shiver going up her spine. If she'd been an animal in the wild, she'd have run for cover immediately because her every instinct was telling her that she was in danger.

"I'm Mr. Livingston's new cleaning lady," she managed to say. "It's my first day on the job."

"Oh. And what were you doing under the desk— looking for dust bunnies?" His voice was a throaty growl, and his icy gray eyes matched that tone.

Good question. Rachel said the first thing that came to mind. "I didn't think anyone was supposed to be here so I got scared when I heard you come in. I thought maybe you were a burglar."

God, could she possibly sound wimpier? She would never convince him to back off if she didn't put up a better front. Rachel hiked up her chin and tried to look as if she belonged there.

It didn't work.

The step that Meredith took toward her put a serious dent in what little fight she had managed to assemble. All she could think of was Jared and the baby. If Meredith was the one who killed Aaron Merkens, then he probably wouldn't show much mercy to Jared or a child.

Rachel caught the edge of the desk to steady herself. The last thing she wanted to do was faint, but by God she felt a dizzy spell coming on. Still, she didn't let that dizziness turn her to mush. She instinctively knew she had to show some backbone or things might quickly get out of hand.

"I'm leaving," Rachel said with authority that she certainly didn't feel. She fought all the old demons, the old fears from her parents' deaths. "I'll come back after Mr. Livingston is at work."

Meredith caught her arm.

Because she had nothing else to rely on, Rachel went on pure instinct. She shoved his hand away and again tried to go around him. She had nearly made it to the patio door before Meredith snagged her arm again. His fingers dug into her skin. It hurt, and she winced in pain.

That did it. Rachel gave up any pretense that this would end with placid requests. "You're asking for a knee in the groin, mister."

Inching his body closer, he trapped her against the door. "Don't you think I know what you're doing?"

As threatening as that sounded, she preferred that to his knowing *who* she was. She hoped he thought she was a thief. Now, the real question was how she could get away from him without Jared having to use his gun.

"It was stupid for you to come here," Meredith insisted. "Dillard didn't do a very good job of protecting his woman, did he? But his stupidity is my gain."

He knew.

God, he knew.

Meredith pushed harder, and Rachel felt the sting of his hand on her arm. She'd have bruises, but she prayed that was all she'd have. It didn't help that he

The Harlequin Reader Service® — Here's how it works:

Accepting your 2 free books and mystery gift places you under no obligation to buy anything. You may keep the books and gift and return the shipping statement marked "cancel." If you do not cancel, about a month later we'll send you 4 additional books and bill you just $3.99 each in the U.S., or $4.74 each in Canada, plus 25¢ shipping & handling per book and applicable taxes if any.* That's the complete price and — compared to cover prices of $4.75 each in the U.S. and $5.75 each in Canada — it's quite a bargain! You may cancel at any time, but if you choose to continue, every month we'll send you 4 more books, which you may either purchase at the discount price or return to us and cancel your subscription.

*Terms and prices subject to change without notice. Sales tax applicable in N.Y. Canadian residents will be charged applicable provincial taxes and GST. Credit or Debit balances in a customer's account(s) may be offset by any other outstanding balance owed by or to the customer.

If offer card is missing write to: Harlequin Reader Service, 3010 Walden Ave., P.O. Box 1867, Buffalo NY 14240-1867

NO POSTAGE
NECESSARY
IF MAILED
IN THE
UNITED STATES

BUSINESS REPLY MAIL

FIRST-CLASS MAIL   PERMIT NO. 717-003   BUFFALO, NY

POSTAGE WILL BE PAID BY ADDRESSEE

HARLEQUIN READER SERVICE
3010 WALDEN AVE
PO BOX 1867
BUFFALO NY 14240-9952

Get FREE BOOKS and a FREE GIFT when you play the...

LAS VEGAS
GAME

Just scratch off
the gold box with a coin.
Then check below to see
the gifts you get!

YES! I have scratched off the gold Box. Please send me my **2 FREE BOOKS** and **gift for which I qualify.** I understand that I am under no obligation to purchase any books as explained on the back of this card.

381 HDL DUYN   181 HDL DUY4

FIRST NAME	LAST NAME

ADDRESS

APT.#	CITY

STATE/PROV.	ZIP/POSTAL CODE

(H-I-03/03)

Visit us online at
www.eHarlequin.com

7	7	7	Worth TWO FREE BOOKS plus a BONUS Mystery Gift!
🍒	🍒	🍒	Worth TWO FREE BOOKS!
🔔	🔔	☘	TRY AGAIN!

loomed over her and outweighed her by a good seventy-five pounds.

She could feel the rage in him. And he was ready to unleash it all on her. Since this could easily turn into a fight for her life, Rachel lunged for a glass paperweight on the desk.

Meredith beat her to it, and knocked it out of reach.

Rachel tore herself away from him, but before she could put some distance between them, he latched onto a handful of her hair. With seemingly no effort Meredith shoved her face-first against the wall.

"You really shouldn't have done that," she said through clenched teeth.

She hadn't wanted to fight him, but she wouldn't stand there while he beat the heck out of her, either. Rachel pivoted, fully intending to send his reproductive organs right into his throat, but with a flash of motion, he drew his gun.

And aimed it right at her.

Her reaction was instant. Something she couldn't stop. Something beyond fear. Something raw, primal and totally beyond her control. Rachel felt every muscle in her body turn to iron. Her breath froze in her lungs.

Move, she ordered herself. *Do something.*

But she couldn't. Her feet wouldn't cooperate. Neither would the rest of her body. Only her mind seemed to be functioning at full capacity, and all she could do was stare at the gun.

That thin black chamber.

The glint of the morning sun on the metal.

Meredith's finger on the trigger.

He probably wouldn't kill her. Because he needed her alive to testify. But from that cold look in his eyes, she had no doubt that he would hurt her. Rachel fought a silent battle. She had to move. She had to save herself.

Meredith suddenly snapped backward. She heard the slam of muscle against muscle just a split second before she saw Jared. He rammed his fist into Meredith's face and sent the man sprawling.

Meredith cursed and put his hands on the floor, preparing to launch himself at Jared.

"I'd think twice about doing that if I were you," Jared warned. He kicked Meredith's pistol aside and aimed his gun at the man.

Meredith hesitated. He shook his head and slowly started to get to his feet.

"Are you all right, Rachel?" Jared asked without taking his attention off Meredith.

"Yes." She was afraid to say differently. Jared had a dangerous edge to his voice, and Rachel wasn't sure what he would do. "Where's Livingston?"

"Tied up in the bedroom."

So that left just Meredith for them to deal with. Of course, that was more than enough.

As if on cue, Meredith actually grinned at them. He seemed to be on the verge of saying something arrogant, or just plain stupid, but then he shut his mouth. But then, almost anything he said at this point would probably be incriminating.

"You'll regret this, Lieutenant Dillard," Meredith challenged.

"Not as much as you will. I've got nothing to lose, so listen carefully. Don't even think about going for your gun. Instead, do the smart thing and cooperate. Get facedown on the floor and do it now."

The moments seemed endless, but Meredith did as Jared requested. Jared worked fast. He took a roll of clear packaging tape from the desk and used it to truss Meredith's wrists to his feet. In less than a minute, he had Meredith restrained, and they were on their way out the door.

Jared had parked at the end of the street, but he slowed her to a walk when she tried to run. She realized that it would attract too much attention from the neighbors. Still, if anyone took a close look at her face, they'd know that all was not well. She'd just endured one of the most frightening incidents of her life—and what made it so bad was that it wasn't over.

"Are you really okay?" Jared asked after he'd

gotten them in the car and sped out of the neighborhood.

"Yes."

He glanced at her. "Try that answer again, Rachel, but this time leave the B.S. out of it."

"All right. I'm still a little shaky." It was a huge lie. She was a lot shaky, but Rachel tried to keep the moment light, hoping it would soothe some of the anger she saw in Jared's eyes. She didn't want him to lose it, especially since she was already so close to the edge herself. "Meredith really gave me a scare when he pulled that psycho-without-a-cause routine."

"Yes." And he repeated it under his breath. "I don't think he knows how close he came to dying. When I came in that room and saw his hands on you, I wanted to kill him."

Because she knew it was the truth, Rachel touched his arm and rubbed lightly. She only hoped that he didn't notice that her fingers were trembling. That would certainly cast some doubt on her *I'm okay*. "You showed great restraint, considering."

"The day's not over yet. I'm still toying with the idea of going back after him."

"But you won't. It'll only cost us time that we can't afford to lose. Besides, we have to find this Dr. Randall Sheridan. He's the key, Jared. I just know it."

He nodded. "We need to talk to him. I'll call Tanner and get him started on this right away. It's probably not a good idea if we go searching for the doctor in broad daylight, but Tanner's people can locate Sheridan and set up a meeting."

"Yes." Rachel had to take several deep breaths before she could continue. "And Sheridan will lead us to the baby."

This time, Jared didn't nod. But she repeated the words to herself. For reassurance.

They would find the baby and get him to safety, away from people like Meredith. They had to.

Because the alternative was unthinkable.

Chapter Ten

Jared tossed the car keys on the desk and swore liberally. "I never should have taken you to Livingston's house with me. *Never*. I had a bad feeling about the place the second we got there—but did I pull back? No. I let you walk in there and face Meredith."

With each mile that he'd driven to get them back to the hotel, reality had sunk in a little deeper. Just minutes earlier, Rachel had practically been killed, and—damn—it was all his fault.

"Hindsight is such a wonderful thing, isn't it?" she murmured.

Rachel looked the pillar of strength standing there. She had her arms folded over her chest and her eyes focused. She even had her mouth set in that stubborn line. The facade worked, temporarily.

Until Jared glanced at her arm.

"What the hell is this?" He caught her wrist,

shoved up the loose sleeve of her T-shirt and examined the reddish marks on her forearm.

Rachel didn't answer. She didn't have to. Because Jared put it together immediately. And it turned his stomach.

"Meredith did this to you." The cursing reached a whole different level and intensity. "Hell, I can't even protect you while you're in the same house with me."

Rachel pulled her arm from his grip and slid her sleeve back in place to cover the marks. "It's not your job to protect me, Jared. As I recall, you were busy taking care of Livingston at the time. Besides, these are just bruises. They'll go away in a couple of days."

A spark of rage shot through him. "But the memory of that bastard putting them there won't."

"I know," she whispered. "I know."

She sank onto the edge of the bed and folded her hands in her lap. Only then did Jared realize she was trembling. But not just trembling. She was shaking. Hell, here he was ranting and venting, and he had forgotten all about what she might be going through.

He went to her immediately and wrapped his arm around her. While he was at it, he checked her eyes to make sure she wasn't going into shock. She wasn't. But Jared saw things in those green depths that made him want to tear Meredith limb from limb.

"It's over," Jared said softly, hoping his words would soothe her enough to stave off a panic attack. He brushed a kiss on her temple and felt her pulse hammer against his mouth.

"It's never over," Rachel countered. "Any idea how many hours of therapy I've had?" She didn't wait for him to answer. "Too many to count. Plus, the hypnosis and the various medications. You name it and I've tried it. Nothing's worked. I'm still too terrified of guns to protect myself. Talk about a genuine wuss."

"You're not a wuss. You have a phobia. Lots of people do. But that didn't stop you from standing up to Meredith today. I know how much it cost you to do that."

She waved him off. "I don't want your sympathy."

"Good, because this isn't sympathy. This is me telling you that we succeeded this morning. You managed to get the info about Dr. Sheridan, and we both made it out of there alive."

"Yeah, thanks to you. I froze, Jared. When I saw that gun, I was seven years old again. I was right back in that room with my parents' bodies, and I was just as ineffective today as I was then."

"You were a kid when that happened—you were supposed to be ineffective. If you'd tried to confront that burglar, he probably would have used that gun on you.'' The reminder didn't do much to settle the acid churning in his stomach. ''And even with all that baggage from your past, you still didn't have a panic attack today.''

She shrugged. Not a casual, dismissive gesture—every muscle in her body was still knotted. ''I'll repeat what you said earlier about Meredith. The day's not over yet. I still might go medieval on you, so you might want to hold back on those compliments.''

Because there was a slight touch of humor mixed in with all the other emotions, Jared smiled and pushed the hair away from her face. ''No way. Because of you, we'll soon find the doctor. And the baby.''

Of course, that last part was wishful thinking. He'd phoned Tanner with the information on the drive back to the hotel, and he had no doubt that Tanner would find Dr. Sheridan, in time. There was no guarantee that Sheridan would lead them to the baby, but then, there'd been no guarantees of anything right from the start.

Rachel lay her head on his shoulder and slid her arm around his chest so she was holding him. ''Thank you for stopping Meredith and for getting me out of there.''

''No problem.'' He went for a cocky, light tone, hoping it would help. ''Consider it my knightly deed for the day.''

Jared skimmed his fingers over her cheek. Rachel turned, moving into his touch. And he suddenly found his fingertips on her mouth.

They didn't stay there for long.

Just like that, she brushed his hand aside, and Jared saw her eyelids flutter down. That was the only warning he had before her mouth came to his. Not some gentle kiss of reassurance.

Not this.

This was hot and needy. Pure, uncut passion. Rachel wound her arms around him, pressed herself against him and made love to him with her mouth.

Jared took everything she offered. Everything. The silky heat of the kiss. The intimate contact of their bodies. The promise of more. Much more. But then, he felt her hand on his arm.

She was still trembling.

"Rachel," he warned. Somehow, he managed to untangle himself from her. "We shouldn't be doing this."

She stared at him, her breath coming out in short spurts. "Sorry. I thought…well, I just thought…" She shook her head. "Obviously, I thought wrong."

"No. You didn't." Jared started to explain, to tell her that he'd pulled away not because he'd wanted to but because she was responding to leftover adrenaline. But the words didn't come.

"You need to rest," he finally managed to say.

Because he was watching her so closely, he saw the emotions run through her eyes. Not hurt, exactly. Something deeper. Something that sent him reaching for her. Rachel stopped his hand before he could touch her.

They sat there. In silence. Their gazes connected. Jared could still hear her breathing even over the heartbeats that pounded in his head.

"There are rules about this sort of thing," he said. "I can't—"

Jared knew anything he was about to say would be a useless explanation. Rachel knew their situation as well as he did. She was scared—yes. And coming down from a terrible ordeal—definitely. Still, that didn't change what was going on between them now.

It wasn't just adrenaline he saw in her response. He saw heat. The same need that he felt racing through his body. Too bad their mutual needs were racing in the same general direction.

And it was really too bad that he wasn't going to do a thing to slow them down.

There would be hell to pay. No doubt about it. But Jared figured whatever the price, it'd be worth it. After all, this was Rachel.

RACHEL WAITED FOR Jared to give her another get-some-rest snarl.

That didn't happen.

Instead of a snarl, Jared reached out and laced their fingers together. Gently.

"Jared?"

It wasn't even close to a warning, but he didn't let her finish, anyway. He pressed his fingers to her mouth and shook his head. "If you're planning to stop me, Rachel, do it now."

That warning wasn't much of a deterrent, and she certainly didn't stop him. Nor would she. Rachel had known that the moment she started this.

Jared settled things. He reached for her and kissed her. It was one of those hard, slow, long ones. One that fed the passion she already felt. The heat seeped from his mouth all the way to her toes.

"Well?" he asked.

"I'm not stopping anything."

Rachel braced herself for a frantic onslaught, for the fire and energy she'd felt during the toga kiss. But Jared surprised her when he gently took her by the shoulders and laid her on the bed. He didn't continue the kiss. Not on her mouth, anyway. Instead, he worked his magic on her neck, trailing a line of kisses to her breasts.

"Let's see if I can remember exactly how to do this," he teased.

Oh, he knew. He knew every inch of her body, and he seemed ready to prove it.

Jared planted her hands on the bed just above her

head. He slid his fingers up her shirt, inch by inch. Because she was watching him so closely, she saw his eyes darken. "You're not wearing a bra."

"It's still drying in the bathroom."

"A convenient place for it." He slid up the T-shirt. "It saves me a step or two."

But it didn't seem as if saving time was a huge priority. Those slow, clever kisses continued at a very leisurely pace. He ran his tongue over her skin. And drove her mad.

When she reached for his shirt, Jared simply clamped onto her hands again. "That wasn't what I had in mind."

"Oh, yeah?" Her breath was thin and shallow now. Every inch of her was humming from antici-pation. "So, what exactly are we doing?"

She should have known that he wouldn't skirt around a challenge like that. Jared unbuttoned her jeans and stripped them off her. Her panties soon followed. And then he showed her what he had in mind.

Jared placed one very wet kiss on the inside of her thigh. The upper, upper inside. A place where his hot breath was just as arousing as the kiss. Then, he latched onto her hips and put his mouth to work right on the feverish center of her body.

Rachel almost jumped off the bed.

"Come here," Jared murmured, his voice a gruff

whisper. ''Let's do something that doesn't have a thing to do with stopping.''

Rachel quickly realized he planned to finish what he'd started. While the idea greatly appealed to her, she wanted more. ''I prefer making love to be a mutual satisfaction kind of thing.''

''Don't think for a minute that I won't be enjoying this. I will.''

She tried to go after his zipper, but Jared stopped her by gripping her wrist. He kissed her, stealing her breath.

Rachel managed some profanity. Nothing that even she could understand. But then, words weren't needed. The way he used his mouth said it all, and her response let him know that. She slid her leg over his shoulder, pressed herself closer to his mouth and just took what he offered.

Jared was very good at offering.

He kissed. Nipped. Used his tongue until the pleasure closed around her. Rachel grabbed onto handfuls of the sheet, trying to anchor herself.

She felt the upward spiral start. The rise. The swirl of sensations so immense, so right that her body could hardly contain it.

Then, Jared somehow took her even higher.

He savored her, and let her know that this gave him as much pleasure as it did her, even though Rachel thought she could argue that case later. And when he was done with her, when she could take no more, he gave a clever flick of his tongue and sent her flying. In that last desperate second, she called out his name.

Jared gave her some pleasant aftershocks with a few more of those well-placed kisses. Still, Rachel forced herself to come back to earth as quickly as possible so that she could return the favor.

With her body still trembling and her breath racing, she held Jared's shoulder to get him moving in the right direction, but he stopped her again.

A groan escaped from deep within his chest. He took her hand, kissed it and moved off the bed. Out of her reach. He walked to the other side of the room, turned and looked at her.

"Get some rest, Rachel."

"Hold on." She didn't intend to let him get away that easily. "Are you saying that you're not going to join me on this bed?"

He nodded. Not easily. But it was a nod. "It's for the best."

"Says who?"

"Me," he clarified.

It was some clarification, all right. And it riled her. "I know what you're doing, Jared. You've given me some great sex, but what you haven't given me is yourself."

He stared at her. "What the hell does that mean?"

''I repeat, you gave me *great sex*. Still, you're holding back. You figure if you don't make love to me—really make love to me—if you only give instead of take, then you'll be able to stop yourself from getting too close to me again. It doesn't work that way.''

He groaned again and pressed the back of his head against the wall. ''I know what's happening between us, damn it, but I also know it's something that'll have to wait. We have too many things to work out first for us to get into a discussion about our future.''

True enough. There were more obstacles than she cared to consider. But even the obstacles couldn't make her put aside what she felt for Jared.

No.

She was falling in love with him all over again, and that scared Rachel almost as much as the other obstacles they faced. But admitting that to herself didn't do a thing to help answer one huge question.

What was she going to do about it?

Chapter Eleven

Clarence Esterman ran his fingers over his slender gold ink pen and read through the letter that his attorney had just handed him.

"When did you receive this?" he asked Lyle Brewer.

"Less than an hour ago. Your assistant, Gerald Anderson, dropped it off at my office since you weren't allowed personal visitors today. I figured it was important so I brought it right over."

Oh, it was important. Critical, even. And it angered him to the point that Clarence's hand tightened. He snapped the expensive gold pen in half and cursed when the black ink oozed over his fingers.

Brewer quickly handed him a handkerchief, causing the guard on the other side of the glass doorway to take a step inside. "A problem?" the guard inquired.

Clarence gave him a sappy, sweet smile that no

one could have interpreted as sincere. ''Not unless you consider shoddy manufacturing something that'd concern you. They don't make pens like they used to.''

The guard cast uneasy glances at both men before he went back to his original position and shut the door between them. With that distraction out of the way, Clarence returned his attention to the letter.

So, Lieutenant Dillard had made the connection to Dr. Sheridan. It was a tough break.

Especially for the doctor.

Randall Sheridan had been prompt about repaying his debts, but he wasn't indispensable. Quite the contrary. He was a loose end in desperate need of elimination. Measures should have been taken days ago to do away with him. Soon, Clarence would personally find out why they hadn't been.

Clarence reached over and plucked the pen from his attorney's hand. Best to make this direct. And cryptic. After shredding all those incriminating documents, he certainly didn't want to give the prosecution anything they could use against him.

He jotted down a couple of key phrases at the bottom of the so-called report. Instructions that Gerald would have no trouble interpreting. By noon, the doctor would be dead, and Lieutenant Dillard would be receiving a rather nasty ultimatum.

Clarence refolded the single sheet of paper, inserted it into the envelope and sealed it. "It's best that you're not involved in this," he told Brewer, when his attorney cast him a questioning glance. Clarence handed him the envelope. "You'll take that to Gerald Anderson immediately. He'll know what to do with it."

Brewer nodded. "There was one other thing—"

He paused, his mouth thinning and his Adam's apple bobbing. Clarence knew the man well enough to know that something was bothering him.

"I spoke with the DA this morning, and he mentioned that you'd asked to have a private conference with him."

If Clarence had had another pen, he would have crushed it into a thousand pieces. Apparently, confidentiality meant nothing to the district attorney. It was a serious error in judgment on both his part and the D.A.'s.

"I wanted to discuss this latest trial delay," Clarence lied. He calmly handed Brewer the ink-soiled handkerchief. "I believe the expression that applies here is fish or cut bait. In other words, I'm entitled to a speedy trial and I want that trial to progress with or without Rachel Dillard and her so-called testimony."

The attorney shrugged. "We've been granted four delays during the past year. This is the first one for the prosecution. The DA will toss a request like that in your face.''

''Perhaps. But it does no harm to ask.'' Or to offer. And by God, he had plenty to offer. But that was something he'd keep between the district attorney and himself.

Maybe it wasn't too late to save himself. Of course, that would mean throwing his partner—along with a few other insignificant employees—to the dogs.

No matter.

There were certain things that just couldn't be helped. Right now, he had to focus all his attention on the Dillards.

JARED STEPPED INTO the steamy shower and let the hot water pound against him. It didn't help ease the throbbing pain in his head and neck.

Nor did it ease anything else that was throbbing.

What it did do, however, was give him a little time to think. It didn't take him long to reach the conclusion that his judgment was sorely lacking in a couple of critical areas.

He was batting a thousand today in the stupidity department. First, he'd ignored all kinds of primitive warnings—warnings that had saved his butt on too many occasions to count. Yet, he'd pushed them aside this time, and it had gotten Rachel hurt at Livingston's house.

Then, as if that incident weren't enough to throw things into turmoil, he hadn't kept the latest comforting session at the cuddle-and-kiss level. Oh, no. Not him. He'd made love to her under the guise of helping her overcome her ordeal.

Yeah, right.

That'd been part of it, of course. A major part. However, somewhere around the time he'd gotten her on that bed and stripped off her clothes, the thought of helping her overcome her ordeal had gotten significantly overshadowed by the thought of some great oral sex.

He hoped that had relaxed her—even if it had done the exact opposite for him. Being with Rachel had caused a frenzy in his nether regions. So far, the shower wasn't helping. Nor would it. A shower couldn't cure that kind of discomfort.

Jared heard the bathroom door open, but before he could even turn off the water, the vinyl curtain slid back. Rachel stood there, the phone in her hand. She didn't avert her attention from his totally naked body. In fact, she slid her gaze down the length of him. It was a challenge. A sexual gauntlet.

That would have to wait.

She handed him the phone. "It's Tanner."

"Thanks." But he was talking to the air, because Rachel had already turned and walked away.

Even though he obviously had some unfinished business with Rachel, he welcomed the call. He hoped it was the news he had been waiting for. News that would ultimately lead to a showdown. Him against whoever the hell had the baby. His only regret was that Rachel would have to be there to witness it. He didn't want her in any more danger, but he couldn't see a way around it.

"You have something for me?" Jared asked. He wrapped a towel around his waist and stepped out of the tub.

"Yeah. I tried to call about fifteen minutes ago, but your line was busy."

"Busy…" He'd been in the shower for the past fifteen minutes. Jared shrugged it off. Rachel had probably had the cell phone tied up with the computer modem.

"I managed to get an address for Dr. Randall Sheridan," Tanner explained. "That's the good news, but the bad news is he's not there. I sent one of my people through the house. Just a cursory look. No signs of a baby or anything else."

Jared hadn't expected a smoking gun. However, he had expected to speak to the man, and soon. "What about his office?"

"Office*s*. He has two of them. We came up empty

there, too. Sheridan has a private practice, but he mainly works at a downtown clinic that caters to the poor and uninsured. He didn't show up for work this morning, even though he was scheduled to come in nearly an hour ago. The staff is worried. They say it's not like him to miss work without calling.''

"Hell." Had Esterman's people already gotten to the doctor—to silence him?

Tanner must have come to the same conclusion. "I've put every available man on this. If the doc is alive and in the area, we'll find him. And as soon as we locate him, I'll see what I can do about setting up a safe meeting. No repeats of what happened at Livingston's.''

That was the critical part. He couldn't put Rachel through that again. "I really owe you for this.''

"You bet you do. Don't worry, that pound of flesh won't hurt too much when I collect." Tanner paused. "There's more. I'll start with the simple stuff and work my way up. Dr. Sheridan is a parolee. A fairly recent one. He was in jail because of a DWI that resulted in some pretty serious injuries. He was supposed to serve three to five years, but he got out after fourteen months. Guess who helped him to secure an early release?''

"Esterman."

"You got it."

It wasn't much of a surprise, and it went a long

way toward convincing Jared that Dr. Sheridan was the man they were looking for. Jared hoped the doctor was still alive, so he could help them.

"Maybe we should carry this parole thread a little further," Jared suggested. "I'll have Rachel do a computer search for someone that Esterman could have hired to take care of the child."

"You mean like a nurse?" Tanner asked.

"Yeah. Or maybe a nanny or a day-care worker. If Esterman got the doctor from prison, maybe he did the same thing with the caregiver."

"Then, that leads us back to Warden Livingston. You think he's Esterman's partner in all of this?"

"Could be. But that doesn't rule out Sergeant Meredith or the attorney, Lyle Brewer." Jared cradled the phone against his shoulder and dried his face with a towel. "Maybe all three are Esterman's silent partners."

"Did you get a feel for that when you spoke to Livingston at his house?"

"No. We didn't actually *speak*. When he walked into the closet to change, I put him in a chokehold, wrestled him to the floor and tied him up. I don't even think he got a good look at me."

Not that it mattered. While Jared was doing all of that, Meredith was assaulting Rachel in the other room. He should have just clubbed Livingston and gotten to her immediately. It would have saved her from going through that ordeal.

"I guess it's time to go another rung up that information ladder." Tanner blew out an audible breath. "I had the DNA tests walked through for you, and the lab just called me with the results."

That drew Jared right out of his thoughts about Livingston. With everything else going on, he'd almost forgotten about the DNA results. Yet, those results were critical for Rachel's and his future.

"Are you still there?" Tanner asked.

"Yeah." Jared cleared his throat and tried to brace himself. "Tell me what you have."

"What I have is a match for the kid, Jared. Sorry to just toss it out like this, but he's yours. Yours and Rachel's."

Chapter Twelve

Jared hadn't anticipated that the news would feel a whole lot like a punch to the gut.

But it did.

It felt like that and more.

The photograph flashed in his mind. The tiny innocent baby. *His* baby. A baby that was in the worst kind of danger.

A sickening feeling hit him so hard that Jared had to lean against the sink. It wasn't every day that a man learned he was the father of a child he'd never even seen. A child that he could easily lose.

"Are you okay?" he heard Tanner ask.

"Not really." He let go of the sink and leaned against the door. He didn't want Rachel to walk in and see him like this. He had to get control of himself. "Just how accurate is that test?"

"It's like that soap commercial—it's ninety-nine point nine percent."

Yeah. That's what Jared figured. Tanner wouldn't have told him the news, otherwise. "I have to go. Rachel needs to know this."

"Sure. I understand. I'll get back to you as soon as we locate the doctor."

Suddenly, that search took on an even greater urgency. And so did the tight fist that had hold of his heart. Hell, he couldn't protect Rachel or his child. Yet, he had to. Somehow, he had to keep them safe.

Jared dressed quickly. He certainly didn't want to deliver the bombshell to Rachel while he wore nothing but a damp towel. He'd barely gotten his jeans zipped, however, before she tapped on the door.

"What'd Tanner want?" she asked.

He told her the part about Dr. Sheridan while he put on his shirt. But there was no way he wanted that door between them when he told her about the baby.

Wishing for a double shot of whiskey, Jared took a deep breath instead and opened the door. Rachel was right there. Waiting. And she immediately studied his face.

"Something's wrong," she concluded.

"Sit down." He took her by the arm and led her to the bed.

She shook her head. "If it's bad news about the baby, then sitting won't help. Just tell me what Tanner found out."

"It's not bad." Well, not in the strictest sense of

the word it wasn't. It just made everything a lot more personal. And more urgent. ''Tanner got the DNA results.''

''Already?'' She stared at him for several moments, obviously looking for clues as to what he knew. ''I think I'd like to sit down now.''

He nodded. Jared felt the same way. He sank onto the bed beside her, eyes fixed on the floor and tried to grasp the enormity of what they'd just learned.

He couldn't.

Best to say it fast because there was no easy lead-in for news like this. ''The child is ours, Rachel. The tests are almost one-hundred percent accurate. We have a son.''

A SON.

Rachel slowly let that sink in. A baby she'd never carried inside her. Never held in her arms. Never even seen. And yet, he was already there in her heart.

Tears threatened, and she hurried to the chair where Jared had left his jacket to pull the photograph from the envelope. Despite her watery eyes, the image suddenly seemed so much clearer.

And more painful.

She had a child, and Esterman's people might hurt him before they could find him.

''I'd given up hope of ever having a baby,'' she admitted. She ran her fingers over the picture. ''Especially when you refused to let me use the embryos after we separated.''

''Yes.''

That was it. The sum total of Jared's response. But Rachel didn't hold it against him. She wasn't sure how she was supposed to respond, either. Most couples had nine months to build up to a moment like this. Nine months of hoping, planning and dreaming.

Their dream was one big nightmare.

''We have to find him,'' Rachel mumbled. She stood and went to the desk. There was nothing to arrange other than two pens and some paper. She settled for that. ''We have to get him away from Esterman. We have to bring him…''

She almost said *home* before she realized she had no home. Not anymore. In a sense, Esterman had taken that from her, as well.

''Let's walk through this,'' Rachel insisted, trying not to panic. But she could feel the panic so close to the surface. ''I need to know what we're going to do. I mean, I know we have to find our child. Then, the next step is, we'll go to the cops and explain why we've been on the run. You'll get to keep your badge, and I'll testify against Esterman.'' She turned around and faced Jared. ''And then what?''

He shrugged. ''Then, we find Esterman's partner and put him behind bars, as well.''

Yes. But what Jared didn't say was that that might

not happen. They might never find this other person. And that meant she'd never be safe.

Nor would their son.

So, they were back to square one, a place Rachel was very tired of being. With Esterman's partner on the loose, she and the baby would likely have to go into the Witness Protection Program. A new life and a new identity. But that left her with one huge question—

What about Jared?

"Just take it one step at a time," Rachel heard him say. "That's all we can do."

Sound advice. But it was also impossible to embrace. She might be a new mother, but her instincts were screaming for her to protect her child.

"Why don't you go back online and search for information on Dr. Sullivan?" Jared suggested. "You might find something that Tanner missed. Also, I think it's a good idea for you to look for recent parolees that Esterman could be using as a nanny."

She knew he was trying to distract her, to get her mind on something productive. And he was right. Worrying would accomplish nothing. Too bad it felt impossible to do what was sensible.

She plowed her hands through her hair and groaned. "He could be right under our noses, Jared, and we wouldn't even know it."

''I know, but I'll do whatever it takes to find him,'' he promised.

She believed him, but what worried her was that that might not be enough. Whatever they did might not be enough, and that was too painful to accept.

''We can't give up,'' Jared added, as if reading her mind. ''If we do, Esterman wins.''

Yes, and their son would lose. It was the right thing to say, to get her moving in a more constructive direction. She wouldn't let Esterman win this one. Not when her child's life was at stake.

Rachel took one last look at the photograph, put it back in the envelope and got to work.

Chapter Thirteen

"Four names," Rachel murmured.

Sitting next to her, Jared read through the information on the computer screen. All four people were recent parolees. All were released with Clarence Esterman's assurance to the parole board that the four would have gainful employment through his company. Any one of the four could be the caregiver for the baby.

Or none of them.

In other words, nothing definitive yet. Maybe Dr. Sheridan could help them in that area. If he was still alive, that is. And if Tanner's people could actually find the man. It'd been nearly three hours since Jared had spoken to Tanner, so obviously they were having trouble locating Sheridan.

Not a good sign.

"That's it—just four names?" he asked. "I was worried there might be more."

''There might be. I went for the obvious so I could narrow down the search. They're all female, none over the age of seventy. None of them have any serious health problems. Two of them are nurses, one was a licensed child-care provider, and the other has some day-care experience. I think these are our best bets.''

''Can you go ahead and get current addresses on all of them?''

Rachel nodded. ''I already have them for the first three, but there isn't anything recent for this one.'' She tapped the last name on the list: Agnes Mc-Cullough. ''I've checked property listings, employment records, Internet listings, you name it. She's just not there.'' Rachel paused. ''But then, if Esterman's managed to get to Dr. Sheridan, maybe he's also gotten to anyone else who could incriminate him.''

True. But Jared tried not to dwell on that depressing thought.

''Esterman isn't perfect,'' he reminded Rachel. While he was at it, it was a good reminder to himself, as well. ''You were able to uncover his dirty dealings, proving not only that he's vulnerable but that he's capable of making mistakes.''

And maybe Clarence Esterman would make yet one more mistake that would put him away for good and help them find their child.

Rachel groaned softly and rubbed the back of her neck. It wasn't an ordinary moan, either. It was laced with fatigue and frustration. Of course, she had been staring at that screen for hours while they waited for Tanner's call. Added to that, she'd been working too hard and eating too little. The takeout Chinese food that he'd picked up from across the street was still sitting there on the desk. Unopened.

Jared moved her hand away and took over the neck massage. "You're worrying and thinking too much. Believe me, it doesn't help."

"I know, but I can't seem to make it stop. All these crazy thoughts keep going through my head. I swear, I'll need a padded cell before this is over."

Jared knew the feeling and decided they both could use a little levity. He went for the obvious. "Well, I would distract you with some carnal suggestions, but I figure Tanner will call any minute. I hate getting interrupted while in the throes of passion, don't you?"

It worked. She made a small sound of amusement. Not quite a laugh, but it wasn't one of those frustrated groans. It didn't last, though. A moment later her eyelids floated down, and she shook her head.

"Distract me with something," she whispered, her voice strained. "Please."

It was the *please* that got him right where it hurt. God, he hated to see her like this.

"All right. Here goes." Jared went for the not-so-obvious this time, but it was something that he'd been dwelling on a lot lately. "Remember the first time I kissed you? It was your senior year at the university. We were sitting in my car, just outside your dorm. I reached for you. You reached back. At the end of all that reaching, you were in my arms. Right where I'd wanted to get you all night." He paused a heartbeat. "We fogged up the windows."

Rachel glanced over her shoulder at him. She bunched up her forehead. "Are you trying to distract me or get me hot and bothered?"

Jared smiled, and after the nightmare they'd been through, it felt good to share a light moment with her. "Hell, if you have to ask, I've failed already."

She stared at him and studied him before her face relaxed slightly. "I definitely remember our first kiss. You treated me like…glass. Well, for a second or two, anyway. Then we sort of devoured each other. It was French and fantastic."

Jared suppressed a groan. Her memory was way too good for this distraction game. "Well, that's what hellions like me do to innocent college girls like you." He continued the massage, working his fingers across the tight muscles. "We corrupt them with French kisses, all the while trying to cop a feel or two."

Rachel managed a short-lived smile. "I still dream about it."

So did he. It was pretty darn memorable if after six years he could still remember the exact taste of her. That wasn't all. He could also remember every last detail about how her breasts felt when he closed his fingers around her.

The distraction was working. Well, for Rachel it apparently was. It was giving Jared a whole new kind of distraction to deal with. There was suddenly a three-ring circus going on in his boxer shorts.

"And then the second time you kissed me," she continued, "we were at the lake. You'd taken me out on your friend's boat. It was more than just one kiss, though. More like twenty. It qualified as making out."

"And then some." He'd taken a long, cold shower after he dropped her off at the dorm.

It hadn't helped.

And neither was this conversation. It was probably best if this stopped while he could still walk.

"Come on. Let's try some other way to burn off this excess energy." He stood and braced his hands, palms out, in front of his chest. "Without inflicting any permanent damage, show me what you can do. Give me your best shot."

She stood. Slowly. "My what?"

Another wince. "Okay, bad choice of words. I

meant, give me your best boxing move, and I'll see if I can block it. Remember that part about no permanent damage, though. And no aiming at any part of my body that contains vital organs. Let's go.''

Rachel continued to stare at him. ''You're sure?''

''You bet.'' Well, not really, but this had to be a better way to lighten her spirits than talking about French kissing sessions. ''Let's get the juices flowing with a little one-on-one.''

Even though she still looked uncertain, there was nothing tentative about her maneuver. Rachel gave him a warning signal just a second before she slammed her fists into his palms. First one and then the other. Then she pivoted and thrust her elbow against his hand.

Jared grunted at the force, and he managed a grin. Barely.

''Classic Shaolin attack. The soles of your feet were aligned with your palms. The move wasn't too high to give me an opening,'' he complimented. ''And if I hadn't blocked it, it would have hurt like hell. Okay, let me see if I can stop you. Come at me.''

She did so with no hesitation, her right hand aimed at his face. Jared executed a defensive move of his own, deflecting the blow with his forearm. He pivoted, trapping her hand under his arm and then grabbing her wrist.

Rachel looked up at him, scowled. She came back at him immediately with a sidekick aimed at his midsection. Jared was thankful that she pulled back before impact, or she could have done some serious damage. He deflected the kick with his hand.

"A Bruce Lee move?" he asked, surprised.

She shrugged. "Whatever works. The trainer taught me a variety of techniques for defending myself. I think she did a good job with her instruction."

Obviously. And Rachel had done a good job learning. "This is a little more dangerous than I thought it'd be. Either we'd better try a different distraction technique, or we might have to consider sex, after all. This is starting to feel a little like rough foreplay."

He'd meant it as a joke. A really bad joke. But there was no humor in Rachel's eyes. There was, however, a fire. A scorching heat that had him inching toward her.

Just as the phone rang.

"Tanner always did have lousy timing," he mumbled. Then, "This better be good news," Jared said into the phone.

"I guess it'd qualify as good. For us, anyway. Esterman might not feel the same way."

He went completely still, and any aggravation he felt over the interruption was long gone by the time Tanner made it to the end of his sentence. Jared was almost afraid to voice the conclusion he drew, for fear it would vanish before they could do anything about it.

"You found Dr. Sheridan?" Jared asked.

"Yep. He's not only alive and well, he's with me. Ready to come over here and meet him?"

"You bet." He grabbed the notepad and jotted down the address that Tanner gave him. "I'll see you in about ten minutes."

Rachel quickly grabbed her shoes. "Tanner has Dr. Sheridan?"

Jared nodded but didn't waste any time. He took Rachel's arm and hurried out the door.

Chapter Fourteen

The idea of any kind of foreplay went straight out the window. In its place, Rachel felt another huge surge of adrenaline. Another wave of panic. And some hope. They raced out of the room and to the car.

"Where did Tanner set up this meeting?" Rachel asked as Jared drove away from the hotel. She pressed her foot against the dash so she could tie her shoelaces.

"At Sheridan's private office downtown. It's closed today, so we'll get a chance to talk to him without anyone interrupting us." He paused. "Well, hopefully there won't be any interruptions."

Yes. The memory of the fiasco at Livingston's house hadn't dimmed much. Nor had the nauseating reaction she still had to Sergeant Meredith's attack.

"There won't be a repeat performance like the one

at Livingston's,'' he assured her. ''Tanner's going to stand guard while we're inside.''

That was something, at least. Maybe that meant they could find some answers and get away from there before Esterman's people arrived. And maybe those answers would lead them straight to the baby before another day went by.

And then what?

She settled back against the seat and contemplated that. It was a question that had come to mind at least a dozen times in the past twenty-four hours, but since learning the child was theirs, it'd taken on a new urgency along with new complications. What did the future hold for them?

Through all of this, through the search and the steamy kissing sessions, he hadn't said a word about wanting to be part of their baby's life.

Or hers.

However, Rachel doubted he'd just let her walk away with their child. Besides, her leaving would mean the obvious—that their baby wouldn't be with his father, and *she* wouldn't be near Jared, either.

An ache made its way across her chest and sank right into her heart. Was that too much to hope for, that he would ever want her back in her life?

Maybe.

God, maybe it was.

Rachel saw her reflection in the vanity mirror over

the visor. She watched the cold, hard realization take hold of her face. Jared might never risk loving her again.

Never.

This could possibly be as good as it ever got between them. And if so, she might have to accept the fact that the most she'd ever have of him was his child. A child that they couldn't even raise together.

"You're quiet over there," he murmured. "Are you thinking too much again?"

She tied her other shoelace. "No. Now, I'm obsessing. Seems like a good time for it."

As if it were the most natural thing in the world, he took her hand, brought it to his mouth and brushed a kiss over her knuckles. The gesture was obviously meant to comfort her, but all it did was remind her that there was more at stake here than just their child.

"Have you thought beyond this?" she asked. The question was too vague to make sense, but Rachel thought that maybe Jared would understand.

He didn't answer right away. He concentrated on driving. "It's hard not to think about it."

Okay. That didn't tell her much. She pressed for more. "If I'm in witness protection, what do we do about the baby? I mean, about you seeing him."

She had to choke back a groan. She hadn't intended to be so forthcoming, but skirting around issues definitely wasn't her forte.

"I know what you're asking," Jared volunteered. "And I don't know what to say. It's hard to think beyond now, beyond this visit."

Rachel quietly agreed. But it was also hard *not* to think beyond it—

"This is it," she heard Jared say.

Rachel checked her watch. Barely twelve minutes since they'd left the hotel. She hoped, Tanner had had time to set up security.

Jared stopped the car in the back parking lot of the one-story vanilla-colored brick building. There were only two vehicles in the lot. Tanner's black truck and a white car that must belong to Sheridan. It certainly appeared that they'd have privacy.

The place wasn't in the best part of town, and it was modest by anyone's standards. Either being on Esterman's payroll hadn't been lucrative for the doctor, or else Sheridan was a master of deception. Not good. Rachel was praying that he'd be willing to skip the pretenses and spill his guts.

Tanner was at the back entrance, looking much like the guardian of the gate. He held open the door, motioned for them to hurry inside, and then followed right behind them.

"How did you get Sheridan to agree to this meeting?" Rachel asked.

Tanner shrugged. "Let's just say I made him an offer he couldn't refuse."

And with that ominous response, Tanner directed them into a private office. Sheridan was there, seated behind a desk littered with manila folders and other assorted papers. He had a cup of coffee in one hand and a cigarette in the other.

He wasn't quite what Rachel had expected. He was thin, almost wiry. Stress and worry lines were all over his face. And even though he was probably only in his mid-thirties, his auburn hair had streaks of gray.

Tanner immediately turned to leave. "I'll leave the three of you alone."

The moment Tanner closed the door, Jared walked behind the desk, bracketed his hands on each side of the chair and got right in the doctor's face. "Let's make this quick. Do you have any idea who we are?"

Sheridan nodded.

Rachel released the breath she didn't even know she'd been holding. It wasn't a tell-all confession, by any means, but at least he wasn't going to try to stonewall them.

"And you know why we're here, don't you?" Jared again. But instead of a question, it sounded like a threat.

"I know what you want." Dr. Sheridan turned his hazy blue eyes in Rachel's direction. He crushed the cigarette in an ash tray and slowly blew out the leftover stream of smoke. "I'm sorry, but I can't help you. They'll kill me. You must realize that."

"Do I?" she countered. She walked closer. "Or are you the one who put this plan together?"

"No. Never. It was Esterman."

Jared pulled up a chair, parking it right in front of the doctor. "I need names and information. And I need it now. Where's my son?"

"I don't know," Sheridan answered immediately. "I swear I don't."

"Then, you'd better start telling me what you do know, because Esterman isn't the only one you should be afraid of. As far as I'm concerned, my child is in danger because of you, so that makes your life worth next to nothing." Jared paused just long enough to move a fraction closer. "Convince me otherwise, and you might just get out of here alive."

Normally, the threat of violence would have sent her heart pounding, but it was pounding for a different reason now. Jared was a good cop. She knew that for a fact. If anyone could get answers from Sheridan, it was Jared.

With his hand shaking so much that the coffee nearly sloshed out, Sheridan took a drink before he responded. "I'm sorry for what you're going through. I'm even sorrier that I wasn't able to stop this."

"You can stop it now," Jared pointed out.

"But Esterman—"

"You can go into protective custody. Hell, you should have done that already. Because if we can find you, then Esterman won't bother to keep you around much longer. You're a huge liability to him now, and you're living in a dreamworld if you think otherwise."

That must have sunk in, finally. The doctor glanced at both of them and took a deep breath. "You really believe you can arrange protective custody so I'll be out of Esterman's reach?"

Jared nodded. "Not me personally, but I'll put you in touch with someone who can."

If Sheridan believed that, it didn't show on his face. He gave a heavy sigh as if surrendering to the inevitable. The inevitable in this case being not protective custody but something much worse.

"Esterman's assistant came to me in prison a little over a year ago," Sheridan began. He sat his coffee cup aside and rubbed his hand over his face. "He said he could get me out early if I'd do a surgical procedure. He didn't explain beyond that. He just said that I'd have to keep it a secret, and that it might not be legal."

No surprise there. Many things that Esterman did were illegal. "But you agreed, anyway?" Rachel asked.

"Yes." Sheridan stared down at his hands and repeated it. "Because I would have died if I'd stayed in that prison. I swear, I would have died. I was being threatened by this…thug who had this intense hatred for anyone in the medical profession. He'd already gotten to me twice, and each time I ended up in the infirmary. I knew if I stayed there, he'd kill me."

Even though there were tears in the doctor's eyes, Rachel could feel no sympathy for him. He'd known that he was agreeing to do something illegal before he ever left prison, and in this case, the illegal activity had put others in danger.

"So Esterman got you out early," Jared finished. "And you did the in vitro procedure on Sasha Young—"

"Were there others?" Rachel interrupted. It was something that had bothered her from the beginning. After all, several embryos were stolen from the clinic. "Or was Miss Young the only surrogate?"

Sheridan shook his head. "She was the only one as far as I know, and I think Esterman would have told me if there had been others. I did the surgery here in the office. Not ideal conditions, I can assure you. But it was successful."

Yes. Very. And because of that success, she, Jared and their son were facing this horrible ordeal.

"That's a great start, but keep talking," Jared insisted when Sheridan paused.

"I did the prenatal checkups on Miss Young at

her house. Nothing much more than cursory exams. Then, last week Esterman called me to do the C-section. It was a little sooner than I would have liked, but he insisted.''

Rachel latched onto that right away. God, she couldn't believe she hadn't asked about that earlier. ''The baby was healthy when you delivered him?''

''He was fine. Good Apgar.'' Sheridan glanced in her direction again. ''That's the test we give newborns to evaluate their heart rate, muscle tone and other physiological indicators.''

So her baby was alive and well.

At least, he had been about a week ago.

''Esterman had a backup plan,'' Sheridan continued. ''If for some reason the child didn't survive, he wouldn't have told you. He intended to use the infant's DNA to prove the infant was yours, and he thought that would be enough to get you to cooperate.''

Rachel held onto the desk. That wasn't an easy thing to hear. She'd hated her former boss before this, but after listening to Sheridan spell out Esterman's intentions, her hatred reached a whole new level. If all Esterman had wanted from the child was a DNA sample, then maybe…

But Rachel couldn't even finish the thought. She couldn't let her mind go beyond the moment. She was thankful that Jared was able to continue the questioning.

"After you delivered the baby, did you murder Sasha Young?" he demanded.

"No!" Sheridan's face bleached out to a sickly color. "It was that man, Gerald-something. The one who calls himself Esterman's personal assistant, the one who visited me in prison to tell me about this arrangement. He's really a hired killer, that's what he is. He strangled Sasha before she even came out of anesthesia. You have to believe me, I had no idea that Esterman had planned something like that."

"I'll bet Sasha Young didn't, either," Jared tossed back at him.

"Yes. You're right. She was the innocent one in all of this. She just wanted a way to make some money. She wanted a new life. And instead, she was killed."

Yes, and they had to stop him before he killed again.

"Where's the baby?" Rachel managed to ask.

Sheridan shook his head again. "I honestly don't know. Gerald took him just minutes after the delivery, and I haven't seen either of them since."

"Then, give an educated guess as to where you think Gerald took him," Jared ordered.

The man touched his fingers to his temple and mumbled something as if going through some old information. "I can't say for sure, but once when I heard Gerald talking to Esterman on the phone, I heard him mention a woman's name. Agnes, or maybe Alice. I think she could possibly be the one who's taking care of the child."

"Agnes," Jared repeated. "You have a last name for her?"

"No. I only heard him mention her that one time."

Rachel moved closer so she could whisper to Jared. "I know who she is. It's Agnes McCullough. That's one of the names on the list of parolees. She's an RN, but there wasn't an address for her."

Jared stood, reached into his wallet and extracted a business card. He tossed it on Sheridan's desk amid all the paper clutter. "Call that number immediately after we leave and ask to speak to Captain Elizabeth Thornton."

Sheridan didn't take the card, but he stared at it. "Who is she?"

"My boss. Tell her that you have information about Esterman and that you need to be placed in protective custody. She'll work out the arrangements."

"I'm really sorry about all of this." Sheridan sank his fingers into his hair and squeezed his eyes shut. "I had no idea anyone would get hurt."

"Yeah, right" was Jared's comeback. "You helped a monster put a sinister plan into action, and you figured no one would be hurt? At least with that kind of reasoning, you shouldn't have any trouble rationalizing away the fact you put innocent people in danger—including a child. Guess that Hippocratic oath you took of 'do no harm' didn't mean much when the bottom line was saving your own hide.''

While Jared continued to talk with Sheridan, Rachel opened the door to find Tanner waiting on the other side. ''We need to find a woman named Agnes McCullough,'' she relayed. ''She's the one who might have the baby.''

Tanner immediately took out his cell phone, punched in some numbers and repeated the woman's name to whoever had answered. She hoped it was someone with better contacts than she had. She'd had no luck finding out anything on the computer.

''I did a pretty thorough database search back at the hotel,'' she told Tanner when he finished the call. ''But I wasn't able to come up with an address.''

''Then, we'll have to do some hands-on searching. My advice is for Jared and you to lay low until you hear from me. Once Esterman figures out that we've found the doctor, he'll be gunning not just for Sheridan, but for Jared, as well.''

Tanner was right, of course. There was no reason for Esterman to want Jared alive. However, there were some serious reasons why Esterman would want him dead.

"Esterman might do anything to keep you alive, but that courtesy doesn't apply to anyone else in the middle of this." Tanner kept his voice low. Almost a whisper. "In his sick mind, Esterman probably figures if he takes Jared out, you'll surrender. Remember that, when and if all of this comes to a showdown."

Rachel tried to grasp the reality of that. It wasn't easy. She'd known that Jared was in danger, but it sent her heart pounding to hear that threat spelled out.

"Did you hear what he said?" Jared asked, walking up behind her.

It took her a moment to realize that he was speaking to Tanner and not her. Rachel heard the two discuss their options for finding Agnes McCullough, but it was white noise. Background that she had to push aside so she could think.

Remember that, when and if all of this comes to a showdown.

Oh, she would remember, all right.

Rachel was sure of that.

Finding Agnes and the baby was critical. But so was keeping Jared safe. Staying alive so she could testify against Esterman would mean nothing if she lost Jared and the baby. Nothing.

Chapter Fifteen

Jared stood just inside the back entrance to Sheridan's office and watched Tanner drive away. With luck, Tanner's P.I. staff would be able to find Agnes McCullough pronto. And with even more luck, maybe she'd have the baby with her.

"What now?" Rachel asked.

Well, it certainly wasn't what Jared wanted to do. He wanted to get his hands on Agnes *now*. He wanted the baby *now*. But apparently, that wasn't going to happen.

"I guess we go back to the hotel and wait." He stepped out and checked the area to make sure it was safe. Only then did he motion for her to follow him to the car.

Even with everything else going on, he couldn't help but notice that Rachel had been awfully quiet since their conversation with Sheridan. Too quiet. Maybe all of this was starting to get to her. But if so, Jared prayed she could hold it together a little longer. He didn't want to tell her that the worst was probably yet to come.

They had barely made it halfway across the parking lot when he heard the sound. It registered immediately.

A shot.

Just one.

But it was more than enough to make Jared draw his own weapon, and to send them running for cover. It was too far to make it back to the office and too far to the car. So, he gripped Rachel's arm and pulled her to the ground next to Sheridan's vehicle.

She moved closer so she could whisper in his ear. "Was that what I think it was?"

"Afraid so."

She groaned softly, and he pushed her behind him. They waited. In silence. Even though he could hear Rachel's breathing coming out in short spurts.

"Do you see anyone?" she asked.

Jared shook his head. The sound had come from behind them. Not good. Because behind them was the office. Right where they'd just left Sheridan.

"It was a handgun," Jared said, more to himself than to Rachel. "Or else a rifle chambered for a handgun."

"That makes a difference?"

All the difference in the world, and that difference

wasn't good. "If it's a rifle, it means someone probably shot into the building."

"As opposed to someone who was already inside," Rachel finished.

Yes. Either way, Jared damn sure didn't want a rifle-toting assassin to fire shots at Rachel. Or Sheridan. It was possible the doctor could still help them find Agnes McCullough.

While keeping a vigilant watch around them, Jared pressed in Tanner's number. It was a risk. A big one. If the gunman heard the phone ring, he might turn the gun on Tanner. Still, Jared had enough faith in his friend. Tanner had probably already taken cover and was waiting for Jared's situation report.

"I heard the shot," Tanner said the moment he answered. "Are you all right?"

"For now. Did you see anything?"

"No. I'm at the front of the office. Some cars have passed, but no one's stopped."

"Same here. I don't have a visual on anyone. Could the gunman have gotten inside the place when Rachel and I were going out the back?"

"Negative. I had men posted at the front door and the side. They left less than a minute ago."

Less than a minute ago was just about the time that he'd heard the shot. Jared checked the area again and was about to tell Rachel they'd have to make a dash for the car. But something stopped him. The dull heat in the back of his head. A tightness in his stomach.

Something beyond the obvious was wrong.

Levering himself up just slightly, Jared looked on the roofs of the surrounding two-story buildings. It was just a glimpse. A glint of reflected sunlight.

A rifle.

Hell.

Jared didn't waste any time getting that information to Tanner. "The shooter's on the roof of the brownstone. I need a distraction so I can get Rachel out of here."

Tanner didn't answer for several moments. "I see him." He mumbled a curse. "He's got a scope. If he's after you, the second you try to drive out of here, he'll have you in his range and pinned down. The windows on the car aren't bullet resistant."

That meant going back into the building. It wasn't exactly Jared's first choice of escape plan. He needed to get Rachel the hell away from there. If someone nearby had heard the shot, they might already have called the police. Not good. Still, he couldn't risk some stray bullet going through the car window and hitting her.

"We can't stay around here long. Think you can manage to have our shooter off that roof in under ten minutes?" Jared asked Tanner.

''I'll try. Get Rachel in the office and stay down until I give you an all-clear.''

He handed Rachel the phone so he could keep his hands free. ''Come on. We have to go back in.'' Jared positioned her between the gunman and him, hoping that was enough. ''If something goes wrong, get inside. No matter what.''

''Excuse me?'' She pulled him back when he started to move. ''I should be the one protecting you. They don't want me dead.''

No way would that happen. ''We don't know that for sure. They're making up the rules as they go along. Just like we are.''

''Then, why do you have to be the one in the line of fire?'' she asked.

''Because I'm bigger.'' It was a weak answer, but he didn't want to waste any more time arguing a point that wasn't open for debate. ''Let's go.''

He didn't give her a choice. Jared looped an arm around her waist and got her moving back toward the office. His heart pounded harder with each step. No more shooting. Thank God. He didn't know if that was because Tanner had managed to distract the gunman or because the guy was just waiting until he had a better shot.

Jared opened the thick metal door and pulled Rachel inside with him. ''I swear this will make a praying man out of me yet,'' he mumbled.

Rachel started to back into the hallway that led to Sheridan's office, but Jared caught her again and re-positioned them so he was in front. If by some chance Tanner was wrong and a gunman had managed to get inside, he didn't want Rachel coming face-to-face with him.

Jared kept his footsteps light so he could hear any movement in the other room. But it was silent.

"Dr. Sheridan?" he called out.

Nothing.

This wasn't good. The man knew the sound of his voice and should have responded. If he was capable of responding, that is.

Jared had already anticipated what he might see long before he got to the doorway.

And he was right.

Dr. Randall Sheridan was slumped over his desk. Facedown. His lifeless eyes staring at the wall.

There was blood. Plenty of it. But that wasn't what captured Jared's attention. It was the gun still cradled in Sheridan's limp right hand.

The doctor had found a way to avoid Esterman's wrath, after all.

RACHEL GASPED WHEN she saw the body and quickly turned her head away. She wasn't quick enough. In that glimpse, she saw what remained of Dr. Sheridan.

She clamped her teeth over her bottom lip to stop herself from screaming.

Jared motioned for her to stay put, but he walked closer and checked for a pulse in Sheridan's wrist. "I guess he decided against protective custody..."

When he didn't finish, Rachel followed his gaze. Sheridan's phone. It was off the hook, lying on the desk. Jared put his ear closer, listened and then cursed.

"Captain Thornton?" Jared said. "Sheridan called you?"

Rachel couldn't hear the captain's response, but it couldn't have been pleasant. Nor was it short. The woman seemed to be explaining something. Or rather, ordering Jared to do something. Jared's eyes narrowed, and he aimed that narrowed glare at her.

Oh God. Not this. Not now. Rachel definitely wanted to put off this particular confrontation, but from Jared's glare, she could see that wasn't possible.

Jared didn't pick up the phone, but instead he used the end of his key to press the speaker button—perhaps so he wouldn't mar any possible evidence; this was now essentially a crime scene. Still cursing under his breath, he went to the window, lifted the blinds a fraction and peered out.

"Well?" the woman on the phone asked. That one

word hung in air for a while. ''Cat got your tongue, or are you just wasting my time?''

Rachel recognized the voice. It was definitely Captain Elizabeth Thornton. Jared's boss.

''Sheridan said he was about to kill himself,'' the captain continued when Jared didn't respond. ''He made it clear that Rachel and you weren't responsible. Now, while I'm relieved about that, I'm not pleased with the rest of your actions, Lieutenant Dillard.''

''I know. And I don't have time to explain things. A baby's life is at stake—''

''So the doctor mentioned. Drive to headquarters, and we'll discuss it in detail. By the way, in case you missed the subtle nuance in my tone, that was an order.''

Rachel braced herself. An order. This was no doubt why Jared hadn't wanted to speak to his boss. He knew he would have to disobey her.

''I can't go to headquarters,'' Jared answered. Rachel didn't miss the nuance there. The words were strained. His voice, tight. It matched his expression. ''Not until this is finished.'' And with that, he reached over and clicked off the phone.

Even though Jared didn't say it aloud, there was a bottom line to all of this, and it could cost him his badge.

''Wanta save some time?'' Jared asked.

Since Rachel was pretty sure where this was leading, she stalled. "That depends."

"That comment's not my idea of saving time, Rachel." He tossed her one quick, icy glare before he turned his attention back to the window. "Why did you call the captain this morning and tell her that it was your idea to escape? Jesus H. Christ!" It took him a moment to regain his composure. "You told her that you held me at gunpoint and forced me to go with you."

"Oh, that." Rachel quickly ran through her options, only to realize she didn't have any. Jared wasn't about to let go of something like this. His pit bull instincts had already kicked in. "Okay, but I warn you, this is like the proverbial Pandora's box. Once opened, you might not like what you find inside."

"Try me."

She tried him, all right. Rachel didn't pull any punches. "I didn't want you to lose your badge. Not because of this. I know you're doing this for me."

"I'm doing it for *us*. For our son. And I don't need you to defend my reputation or whatever the hell you thought you were doing, got that? You could have accidentally said something to Thornton to give us away. She could have found us through that phone call."

"But she didn't." Rachel had already geared up

to add more, much more, but Jared put his finger to his lips in a be-quiet gesture.

"Hell. It's Sergeant Meredith," Jared grumbled. "Just what we don't need right now."

She froze. Which was a good thing. It saved her from panicking. "Where is he?"

"I see him on the roof. He's got a rifle."

Forcing herself to move, Rachel made her way past the doctor's body and across the room, but Jared kept her back when she tried to look out the window.

"Are we trapped?" she asked, frightened of the answer. It wasn't just because of Meredith. This was costing them valuable time.

"I'm not sure. Let's give Tanner a couple of minutes to lead Meredith away from here, and then we'll try to get out."

Good. She didn't want to stand around in a room with a dead body any longer than necessary. She was so close to a panic attack that she could taste it.

"Why don't you think of our first kiss?" Jared said, his voice anything but romantic. A moment later, she knew why. "Or else you can think about how I'm going to yell at you for calling the captain."

Well, that was a sure-fire way to stave off a panic attack. Rachel decided to wait to panic, or defend herself.

Jared lifted his head slightly and turned back toward the window. "Listen," he whispered.

But she didn't have to listen hard. She heard the sound immediately. A siren. It wasn't close, but she was positive it was headed their way.

"Captain Thornton must have sent out a unit," Jared explained.

Yet more bad news. It might scare off Meredith, but it put them in danger of being found.

"Let's go," he said.

Together they sprinted down the hallway. He didn't stop when they got to the door. Jared shoved it open, scanned the parking lot and gave her the go-ahead.

"I'll walk out first," he instructed. "If all goes well, follow me. Pay particular attention to that 'if all goes well' part, Rachel. Don't go out there if anyone, including me, is shooting. Got that?"

She nodded and braced herself for the run to the car. Tanner might have distracted Meredith so they could escape, but that didn't mean Meredith hadn't doubled back to come after them. Fortunately, she didn't get a chance to dwell on that theory because the phone rang.

"Answer it," Jared insisted. "It'll be Tanner."

Yes. And perhaps with news that he'd lost Meredith.

But it wasn't Tanner.

"A mutual acquaintance got this number for me," she heard the man say. "No easy accomplishment, I can tell you. The lieutenant obviously values his privacy.''

The voice made her blood turn to ice.

''Esterman.'' Just saying his name took the breath out of her. Rachel had to pause a second. Beside her, she heard Jared ask for the phone, but she ignored him.

She covered the mouthpiece. ''Concentrate on getting us out of here,'' she whispered to Jared. ''I'll take care of this.''

Jared objected. As she knew he would. But Rachel disregarded him.

''What do you want?'' she asked Esterman.

''Let's see—what do I want?'' he repeated, his tone cold. ''I want you to do as you've been told.''

Rachel didn't back down. ''And I want my son.''

''Yes. I can only imagine. Your own flesh and blood, and yet you've never even seen the little fellow. He has good healthy lungs, from what I understand.''

God, he would use something like that—the suggestion that her son was crying. It tore at her heart— just as Esterman had known that it would. It didn't break her, though. Too much was at stake for her to let him do that.

''I want to see him.'' Rachel silently applauded herself. Her voice sounded calm and steady. Beneath all that calmness, however, her entire body was one raw nerve. "Where is he?"

"In due time. You should be thanking me, you know. After all, this was my plan. I'm the one who's responsible for that child being born. Without me, you wouldn't have your son. The son you've always wanted."

"A son you've threatened to kill," she reminded him.

"Only if you don't cooperate. The choice has been yours all along. But what have you done with that choice? You allowed your ex to sway you in a seriously bad direction. How many more people must die before you do what's necessary? You are responsible for this."

"Wrong. You're responsible."

"Each second you waste is putting your child in greater danger. So far, I've shown compassion. Don't expect that compassion to continue."

And with that, he hung up.

"What did he say?" Jared asked immediately.

She took a moment to gather her breath. "Nothing that we didn't already know. Our son is in danger, and Esterman is the one responsible."

"That really was Esterman on the phone?"

Rachel nodded. Just nodded. It seemed the best response while she kept hold of the emotions that threatened to break free.

"What the hell did he want?" Jared demanded.

"The impossible." Rachel closed her eyes for a second and fought to hold herself steady. "Now, let's get out of here and find our son."

Chapter Sixteen

Rachel paced across the hotel room while Jared finished his conversation with Tanner. A conversation that had been going on since their return from Sheridan's office.

From Jared's reaction, it seemed things weren't going as well as they'd hoped. Apparently, Tanner's people were having trouble coming up with an address for Agnes McCullough. Not that Rachel had expected it to be easy. If Agnes did indeed have the child with her, Esterman had no doubt made certain that she was hidden away.

So Rachel kept on pacing. It didn't help. There was so much explosive energy inside her that she was about to scream. No amount of pacing—or organizing—would help that. She'd already organized any and everything in the tiny hotel room.

With both the doctor and Aaron Merkens dead, Esterman seemed to be a little farther out of her reach. And yet in some ways, that mattered less than it probably should have. All Rachel could think about was finding Agnes and the baby. Only then would she be able to concentrate on Esterman getting what he deserved.

"They're still looking," Jared informed her when he got off the phone. "So is the patrol unit that Captain Thornton sent to the doctor's office. We have to lie low until Tanner can arrange for us to see Agnes McCullough."

"Yes. Lie low. Wait." She drummed her fingers against her crossed arms. "Since you didn't mention screaming, I guess that's out?"

He smiled, but the smile quickly faded. "Unless you can manage to scream without attracting attention. We already have enough attention as it is." He propped his hands on his hips. "But you could use this time to explain why you called Captain Thornton and lied about kidnapping me."

Rachel rolled her eyes. "Sheesh. Of all the subjects we could disagree about, you would pick that one? There are bigger and meaner fish to fry, Jared."

But that wasn't entirely true. Just lately, she and Jared hadn't disagreed about much. In fact, that particular phone call to the captain and his me-Tarzan approach to her safety were the only subjects that had put them at odds.

Interesting.

In the past day and a half, they'd gone through hell together and had somehow mended a few rifts along the way. Here, they'd been separated for over a year, and she'd miraculously found the secret to putting her marriage back together. Too bad it'd taken a crisis of huge proportions to do it. And too bad it might be too late for anything, short of a miracle.

Since Jared still seemed to be waiting for an answer about Captain Thornton, Rachel stopped pacing and faced him. "All right. Here goes. I lied when I said that I called her only to save your badge. That was part of it, but it was just the tip of the iceberg. I did it because I still care about you, and I didn't want you hurt. Especially since you were doing the right thing when you got me out of that safe house."

He paused a moment. "That's admirable, but you risked getting yourself hurt. Kidnapping is a felony, Rachel. Add to that, I'm a cop—it's a wonder that Thornton didn't call in the FBI to come after you."

She shrugged. When she'd started all of this, she hadn't expected to pour out her heart to him. Still, it didn't make sense to hold back now. Somehow, they'd manage to sift through everything and had reached ground zero. "Well, that just goes to show you the depths of my feelings, huh?"

He just stood there and stared at her. Rachel did the same thing. Not necessarily a good idea. With him that close, she had no problem seeing every emotion on his troubled face.

His ruggedly handsome face.

Which reminded her of lots of other things.

Even with that reminder, she didn't move. She didn't back away. The idea that drifted through her mind took hold, and suddenly it was the only thing that made sense.

"I could probably talk myself out of doing this," she warned. "But I figure I'll explode. You'll make a good substitute for a scream."

It was more than that, of course. Much more. Part of her wanted to say that to him, to bare her soul even more than she already had. Best not to complicate things, though. This might be a hard sell to Jared as it was. After all, he was trying to keep some distance between them.

Rachel latched onto the front of his shirt, pulled him to her and kissed him. She kept it short and sweet, but it sure as heck wasn't some lustless peck. And then she let go of him. Satisfied that she'd convinced him she didn't want to argue, or scream, or even bare her soul, she backed up so he could have a chance to escape.

She made it a step.

Just one.

Before he grabbed her wrist and stopped her.

Rachel turned toward him, her shoulder brushing

his. He looked into her eyes. She didn't need to ask his intentions. She could see it. And feel it. She might have been the one to start this, but Jared was more than willing to finish it.

"I don't want to be a substitute for anything," he said.

Rachel nodded. "Believe me, you're not."

That was it—all it took to complete the mutual invitation. He nodded in return and dragged her closer, pulling her into a searing kiss.

His mouth pleasured and coaxed. Teased. Ignited the spark into a full flame. Rachel felt her heartbeat race. Her body grew warm and golden, and she found herself wrapping her arms around him so she could have more.

"Yes," she whispered against his mouth. "Now, this is what I need."

Jared moved her hair out of the way so he could go after her neck. He took that clever mouth to the sensitive little spot just below her ear. "It's the adrenaline that's got you so wired."

"You think so?" She touched her mouth to his jaw and had the pleasure of feeling a muscle jump there. "If you use that line on every woman you kiss, I'll bet it puts a real damper on foreplay."

He didn't stop the assault on her neck. Or her ear. But he made himself crystal clear. "I wouldn't know.

You're the only woman I've been foreplaying with for years.''

She pulled back and looked at him. ''Is that true?'' But Rachel immediately shook her head. ''Never mind. I don't want to hear the answer to that.''

''Sure you do.'' He met her gaze head-on. ''Go for it, Rachel. Ask. You might be surprised at what I have in my version of Pandora's box.''

Maybe. But she didn't want to risk it. There were a lot of things she could handle, but hearing about Jared's sexual escapades wasn't one of them. Rachel went after his zipper, instead.

''Boxes aside,'' she insisted. Now, it was her turn to kiss his neck. ''I think I'd rather just pleasure you. You know, the way you did me.''

Jared pressed his hand over hers to stop her. ''As wonderful as that sounds—and, believe me, it does— what I have in mind is good old-fashioned sex. Something mindless and mutually satisfying. We'll see how far we get before Tanner calls. But first, I want you to ask the question that's obviously been on your mind.''

She studied his eyes, and his expression. Nope, he wasn't about to back down on this, either. If she wanted things to progress beyond the zipper-lowering stage, she had to ask what she really didn't want to know.

''All right. Have you been with anyone else?''

''No.''

No hesitation. No doubt. That was it. Just that one firmly spoken denial.

It was, well, touching. And a little confusing. Fourteen months was a long time, especially for a man who hadn't been able to keep his hands off her when they were married.

His answer might have soothed her ego if Jared had given it a chance.

He didn't.

What he did was take the first step to fulfilling his promise of something mindless and mutually satisfying. Just as on that night outside her college dorm, she reached for him. Jared was faster. He hauled her against him and kissed her.

THIS WOULD NOT BE A LONG leisurely afternoon of lovemaking, but Jared was sure neither of them cared about that.

Those were about the only totally coherent thoughts that made it into Jared's head. This wasn't the time for coherency, anyway. This was about Rachel, and him, and about how much they needed each other.

She fought with his shirt and won. Rachel managed to get it over his head and send it sailing across the room.

''Take me now,'' she insisted.

To prove she was serious, Rachel went after his zipper again. She wasn't careful about what she touched along the way. She slid her hand down the length of him.

And repeated the move.

Several agonizing times.

Her nimble fingers took him from the primed stage to being fully aroused. Not that he'd needed much for that to happen. That *take me now* comment was like water to a man dying of thirst. Jared very much wanted to oblige her.

He managed to peel off her shoes and jeans. Not easy. Not with her working at the same time to free him from his boxers. They both succeeded, somehow, and he backed her against the wall.

He took her mouth again while she wrapped her legs around his waist. Her mouth was as hot and wet as the rest of her. He touched her, because it was what they both needed, and he saw exactly what his touch did to her.

"This won't be safe sex." Jared positioned her, and she wrapped her legs around his waist.

Rachel hissed out a breath when they made intimate contact. "I don't remember asking for safe."

If she hadn't kissed him and thrust the midsection of her body against his erection, he might have considered the double meaning of that remark. But that brief contact made him remember his priorities.

Jared held her in place with his body. Her naked body against his. Her bare breasts against his chest. And he watched her eyes as he took her. Jared slid into that hot, slick heat and gave them both exactly what they needed.

He stilled just a moment. To savor. But the savoring and stilling came to a halt when Rachel started to move against him, and with him.

It didn't take much. The intensity between them didn't allow more, even though Jared wished that it could last a lifetime.

"Fly for me, Rachel."

She did. At the sound of his words, he felt her body close around him. Felt her soar until she reached a shattering climax. Jared was right there to catch her.

Rachel returned the favor.

With the hot primal need driving him, she took and gave her all in that same moment that he surrendered. He saw her face. Just her.

And that was all Jared needed.

BECAUSE HE HAD NO CHOICE in the matter, Jared slid to the floor, taking Rachel right along with him. They were both damp with sweat, and little wisps of her hair were clinging to her neck and forehead. She looked amazing in the afterglow of good, non-safe sex.

"Don't you dare say that you'll regret this," Rachel mumbled.

"I'm feeling a lot of things, but regret's damn sure not one of them."

And to prove it, Jared gave her a kiss that neither of them would forget. He left them both breathless and wanting more.

There was no turning back now. What had happened couldn't ever be dismissed as just plain sex, even if it had occurred in a heated rush against the wall. He and Rachel had made love. And that left him with one troubling question.

What now?

Now that his head was starting to clear, Jared knew this was just the beginning. They had so many issues.

"You've got that look of obsessing on your face. What are you thinking?" she asked.

Jared didn't want to dive right back into what could easily be a depressing conversation. So he went in another direction. "I'm thinking you didn't scream. I'm thinking with just a little encouragement, I might be able to make that happen."

She smiled. Nothing sarcastic. Nothing meant to minimize the moment. It was real. Just like Rachel. Just like what they felt for each other.

"You're bragging," she whispered. She began to nibble on his mouth.

"Am I, now?"

He was fully prepared to back up that claim, but the ringing phone put a stop to it. Without releasing his grip on Rachel, Jared reached up and grabbed his cell phone from the desk. He cleared his throat in case it was Esterman. But it wasn't. It was Tanner.

"We found Agnes," Tanner informed him.

"She's alive?" And Jared held his breath waiting for the answer.

"She was as of this morning. We found her through a credit card purchase, but she's not in San Antonio. She's got a rental house out on an island near Corpus Christi. It'll be about a two-hour drive for you to get there."

Jared was already reaching for his shirt. "We'll leave in a couple of minutes."

"Here's a warning, though—you might have a few problems with accessibility," Tanner continued. "There's a private road and bridge that leads out to the place, but the initial reports are that it's guarded. *Heavily* guarded. So your best bet is to go via boat. I'll arrange for one."

"Good. Any indication that Agnes has the baby with her?"

"Yeah. I'm working on getting us an infrared, but how's this for an indication—one of my people just got off the phone with the clerk at the general store on the mainland near Agnes's house. They delivered some disposable diapers and some formula there just this morning. Oh, and those diapers apparently come in all kinds of sizes, but the ones that Agnes requested were for a newborn.''

"Let's go," Jared told Rachel. He jotted down directions while she dressed.

Two hours. That was it. Such a short amount of time considering all they'd been through already. Still, they couldn't just go barging into the place. It wouldn't be safe for Rachel, or the baby.

"You'll check out the place before we get there?" Jared asked Tanner.

"I'll do my best, but I can't guarantee security on this one. Hard to guard the Gulf of Mexico. Esterman might have patrols out on that water."

True. But that wouldn't stop him. Nothing would. "We'll deal with that when we come to it. See you in two hours."

Chapter Seventeen

Rachel studied the place through the binoculars, while Jared spoke on the phone with someone from a security company. A light went on in the west side of the house, but there was no sign of anyone.

No guards, no Agnes McCullough.

And definitely no sign of the baby.

The house was two-story, white, with massive marble columns fronting a wraparound porch. It was perched in the center of a lush, finger-shaped island. Pretty upmarket for the residence of a parolee with no recent record of employment. Agnes had done well for herself.

It had taken Rachel much of the two-hour drive to verify it, but she now knew that the same corporation that owned Sasha Young's rental house owned this property, as well. In other words, it was connected to Lyle Brewer, who in turn was connected to Clarence Esterman.

They were no longer at the starting point. This house, Rachel knew, was the finish line.

Luck was with them as far as the weather was concerned. There were only a few milky clouds scattered in the sky. The breeze was mild. The waves moved in a gentle slosh around her feet.

The conditions were ideal.

Still, every muscle and every nerve in her body was on full alert. Even *ideal* wasn't much of a guarantee with her child's life at stake.

Once the sun had set—which was only a few minutes away—they'd be able to approach the house via boat under cover of darkness. It was their best bet, Jared had said.

After that, however, all bets were off.

Once they reached the grounds, they would be too far away for Tanner to help them, and well out of reach of any local law enforcement. Which might be a good thing. If Esterman had managed to buy off a cop in the SAPD, perhaps he owned the locals, too.

"It's not too late to change your mind about this," she heard Jared say. He walked up behind her and brushed his fingers over her arm. "You can always stay here with Tanner to make sure no one follows me out to the island."

"I'm going with you," she insisted, still looking for any sign of movement in the house.

Jared didn't argue, maybe because he knew it was

an argument he stood no chance of winning. Her child was in that house, and she was going in after him.

Tanner's phone rang, and he stepped away from the boat to take the call.

"Did you learn anything from the security specialist?" she asked Jared.

"Some. He tracked down the person who did the original system for the house nearly ten years ago. It's pretty basic. Not too many bells or whistles. I should be able to get through it without too much of a problem."

Rachel didn't miss the key bit of information that he left out of his explanation. "Ten years is a long time. What if someone made modifications to the system after it was installed?"

"Then, I'll figure out a way to get through them, as well." Jared took in a long breath. "By the way, if something goes wrong—"

Rachel quickly pressed her fingers against his mouth so that he couldn't finish. "We both know what we have to do. Let's not spell it out."

Jared kissed her fingertips and gently moved them aside. "No doom and gloom predictions. I just don't want you to take any unnecessary chances."

She nodded. "The same goes for you."

Tossing her a you're-stubborn half snarl, Jared took the binoculars from her and had a look at the house. "I think our best bet will be to hide the boat when we reach the island and try to go in through the back. Hopefully, it won't be as well lit as the front."

"What about the infrared read that Tanner's been trying to get?" she asked.

He paused.

"There appear to be four adults," he finally answered. "And either a baby or maybe a small pet. The infrared wasn't conclusive."

She made a sound of acceptance and stared at the house. It was no pet. Rachel knew that with every fiber of her being. It was her son.

"Anyway, we'll go in through the back," Jared continued a moment later. "And we'll try to avoid the guards or whoever else is in there. If the baby's in the house, he's on the second floor. Or, at least, that's what the infrared indicated when it was taken an hour ago."

"Then we'll get the baby, sneak out and hurry back here," she finished. No need to dwell on the dozens of things that could go wrong between now and then.

"Yeah. And by then, Captain Thornton should have arrived. I called her about twenty minutes ago."

Rachel's head whipped up. "Thornton? Why would you call her?"

"To help wrap up things around here. I couldn't

bring her in on this officially. Not with us breaking into the house.''

She got that part. ''That's the real reason we're not bringing Tanner with us?''

''Right. Even though he wanted to come, I need him here. But Thornton, well, that's a different matter. She never would have agreed to anything illegal. By the time she got the search warrants and assembled a team, it'd probably be too late. But I want her here to go in once we've gotten the baby out. I don't want anyone associated with this plan to walk. Thornton can help us with that.''

Rachel carried that through to its logical conclusion. Thornton would arrange the arrests of the people in the house, but Jared's boss would take her in, as well. To testify and to answer any questions about the illegal things she and Jared had been doing to find the baby. Heck, Thornton might even arrest Jared.

So, this was essentially their D day. They had one shot to come out of there with the baby. Just one.

It had to count.

Jared curved his arm around her waist. ''There'll be no turning back once we're on that boat. I really wish you'd stay here with Tanner—''

''I don't want to turn back. And I don't want to stay. I just want this to be over.''

The sun dipped even lower, until only a sliver of

light was visible on the horizon. She held Jared's hand and led him toward the boat.

"Hold up one minute." Tanner slipped his phone back in his pocket and hurried to them. "I could go with you."

"I'd rather you watch that bridge and the shore to make sure no one follows us." He reached in his pocket and pulled out his badge. "By the way, when Captain Thornton gets here, make sure she gets that."

Tanner reached for it, but Rachel latched onto Jared's wrist. "Wait a minute. Why are you doing this?"

"Because it'll save Thornton the trouble of asking for it, that's why."

She shook her head. "You don't know that. I can't believe you'd just hand…"

Jared stared at her when she hesitated. Even in the filmy light, she saw his eyebrow lift a fraction.

"Questions?" he challenged.

"No." But she certainly had some answers. Answers that she'd been asking herself for years. She knew how much it cost him to hand over that badge. Being a cop was one of the most important things in the world to him.

But obviously not the *most* important.

It broke her heart. And made her feel like a genuine fool for ever doubting him. Later, when this was over, she'd tell him that.

While she was at it, she'd also let him know that she'd fallen in love with him all over again.

Tanner took the badge, glanced at it and slipped it into his pocket. "You need any extra weapons?"

Jared shook his head. "I wasn't planning to do a lot of shooting. A quick in and out. If all goes well, we should be back in under an hour."

It was an overly optimistic guess, but Rachel didn't correct him. She said goodbye to Tanner and thanked him when he wished them luck.

Jared started the outboard motor and got them moving. Of course, they'd have to turn off the engine when they got close to the house and paddle the rest of the way, but at least this initial boost of speed would save them some time. Perhaps very valuable time.

Without the sunlight, the water was eerily dark; she couldn't see even an inch below the surface. And the night closed in around them. She hoped that Esterman hadn't put guards on the shoreline. Or worse, on the water itself. The only things she and Jared had going for them were the element of surprise and their determination.

"Let's name the baby," she whispered when he turned off the engine. Rachel knew that sounded absurd at a time like this, but it suddenly seemed important. "He's a week old and he doesn't even have a name."

"We used to have that list, remember? I seem to recall that Michael was your favorite."

"Yes." She took one of the oars in the boat, and they started to row toward the shore. "But let's pick something different. Something *we* decide right here, right now. It'll be more meaningful that way."

He shrugged. "All right. How about we name him after your father, Benjamin? Or would that cause too many bad memories for you?"

She gave it some thought. "No bad memories, but I'd like your name in there, too. How about Benjamin Jared? And we can call him—"

"Ben," they finished together.

Rachel managed a smile. "Maybe that's a good sign that we agree on the name?"

"Damn straight."

But if Jared indeed felt that way, the feelings didn't make it to his voice. Rachel heard the concern. The doubt. And even the fear. They mirrored what was going on inside her.

They quietly got off the boat and pulled it onto the shore, hiding it in a thick clump of shrubs. Jared paused a moment and looked around them.

"There doesn't seem to be any perimeter security," he mumbled.

At least, none that created an audible alarm. In

fact, the place was quiet. The only sound was that of the surf and the cry of an occasional seagull.

Rachel followed him across the sandy beach to the back of the house. Jared had been right—it wasn't well lit. Just some spotlights on the patio. No guards in sight, either. That didn't put her at ease. In fact, it did just the opposite. Maybe Esterman had used Agnes McCullough, and this house, as a trap. But Rachel prayed she was wrong.

Keeping close to the wall, they walked slowly around the house. Jared tested the first window they came to. It was locked, and they moved on. He repeated that process three more times before he finally stopped and took out the tiny tool kit from his jacket.

Rachel stood on her tiptoes and peered inside. It was a dining room. Dark. Shadowy. And not a soul around. It also appeared to have easy access to a hallway. Beyond that, she could see the stairs.

"Keep a close watch on the yard while I'm doing this," Jared whispered.

Rachel turned so that she'd have a better view of the massive yard. The scarcity of lighting made it more secure for them, but it didn't help her with her surveillance. The grounds were littered with trees, shrubs and outbuildings. Any one of them could provide a hiding place for Esterman's hired guns or for some well-placed cameras that could be monitoring their every move.

Jared used a tiny glass-cutter to take out a fist-size section of the window, and then he reached in and disarmed the security wires. It likely wouldn't disarm the other windows, but it'd at least give them access to this one.

Taking out his weapon, he held it by his side so she wouldn't easily see it and panic. Rachel appreciated that, but he couldn't do that for long. If they encountered a guard, Jared would almost certainly have to use his gun. She prayed that she could deal with that when the time came.

He climbed in first and had a look around before he helped her through. Unlike the night air, the air in the house was cool, a trio of fans whirling overhead. The place smelled of furniture polish and disinfectant.

Jared went to the doorway. Paused. Looked around. And then motioned for Rachel to follow him. He turned off the light as they made their way down the hall to the set of stairs.

Then Rachel heard the footsteps.

Jared didn't waste any time. He jerked open the door to the storage area beneath the stairs and pulled her inside. It was dark and musky, an indication that it didn't get much use. The last thing they needed was for one of Esterman's people to find them before they even had a chance to search for the baby.

Someone opened a door. Not the one to the closet,

thank God. Rachel heard the *click* of a knob in the hallway. Next to her, she felt Jared's arm flex. Nothing more than the readjustment of a few muscles, but he was obviously preparing himself for a fight.

Rachel's body made its own preparations. Her heart pounded. Her breath became rapid. She refused to let the fear paralyze her, but it definitely had her by the throat. Instead, she tried to channel her energy to her fists in case it turned physical. All that Shaolin training might come in handy, after all.

"I don't see the suitcase," someone called out. A man.

But she didn't recognize the voice. It definitely wasn't Brewer or Meredith.

"Don't worry about it right now. We can look for it later." A woman that time.

Rachel had no doubt that it was Agnes Mc-Cullough.

There was a sudden shuffle on the stairs overhead. Followed by more footsteps down the hall. Nothing frantic. Just two people going about some routine business. The footsteps trailed off to silence.

The seconds crawled by.

Jared eased open the door. Paused for a moment. Listened. Apparently satisfied, he motioned for her to follow him. They made it halfway up the steps before she heard the sound. It was soft. So soft. And yet Rachel knew exactly what it was.

A baby crying.

Her breath stalled in her throat, and she froze. Jared didn't, thank God. He seized her arm and got them moving. They made it to the landing.

Another sound.

Faint but definitely a cry.

Even over the pounding of her own heartbeat, Rachel managed to follow Jared and that sound to a room at the end of the long hall.

The door was open several inches. Like a beacon, pale yellow light seeped out and bled onto the carpet. Jared flattened his back against the wall and inched toward the light.

When they were closer, he braced his right wrist and held the gun in front of him in case he had to fire. Crouching low, he pivoted so he could peek around the doorjamb. Rachel had a look, as well.

No one was there.

Cautiously, they went inside. Jared eased the door shut behind them and locked it. Immediately, he began to search the closet and beneath the bed to make sure they were alone. Rachel didn't help him. She spotted the white wicker bassinet in the corner and raced toward it.

She saw the movement of the blanket. Tiny squirms and kicks against the pale blue fabric. And then she saw his face. He was sucking on his fist and apparently not very happy that it wasn't a bottle.

"Jared," she somehow managed to whisper. "He's here. He's really here."

Too many emotions went through her to try to sort them all out. Besides, it didn't matter. The weight of the world just seemed to melt away.

With her hands trembling and her heart in her throat, Rachel carefully lifted him up, and for the first time held her son in her arms.

Chapter Eighteen

Okay.

Jared took several deep breaths and he watched the miracle unfold in front of him. He'd had a lot of expectations about this moment, but not once had he prepared himself for his mouth going dry and his stomach landing on the floor.

The transformation in Rachel was equally startling. The smile. The look in her eyes. The light in her face. The way she brushed her mouth over the tiny forehead. The simple gesture must have been comforting, because their son stopped crying immediately.

Their son.

This child was their son.

Unsure of what he should do, Jared reached out and gently ran his fingers over the thin mat of brown hair. There was an instant connection. Unconditional love so strong that it nearly brought him to his knees, and it was all aimed at that little bundle who was suddenly studying them with inquisitive gray-blue eyes.

''Welcome to the world, Ben,'' Rachel whispered. ''We're your parents, and we're very happy to meet you.''

It was a moment too precious to cut short, and yet Jared had to push what he was feeling aside and get them the heck out of there.

''Let's go,'' he insisted.

Rachel seemed to be in a daze, so he wrapped his arm around her waist and urged her toward the door. The baby whimpered, the sound loud in the otherwise silent room. Before Jared could worry if the noise would alert Agnes, Rachel put the tip of her thumb into their son's mouth. It soothed him instantly.

''Good idea,'' he told her. Thank God for maternal instincts. So far, his paternal impulses were only focused on one area: escape.

They made it all the way to the stairs before Jared heard something he definitely didn't want to hear. Footsteps and voices. Since they already sounded too close for comfort, he pulled Rachel and the baby into the nearest room and locked the door. The lock wasn't much, but if necessary it might buy them a couple of extra seconds.

Unfortunately, those extra seconds could soon become necessary.

When his eyes adjusted to the darkness, he could see that it was some kind of large storage room, stuffed with old furniture and such. He hid Rachel and the baby behind a stack of boxes, reholstered his gun and went to the window to disarm the security wires.

"Hell," he mumbled, looking out.

There was only a thin lip of roof and then a twenty-foot plunge to the ground below. If that was their only escape route, they were in trouble.

Trouble came a lot sooner than he'd anticipated.

"He's gone!" someone yelled. A woman. Agnes, probably. It hadn't taken her long enough to figure out that the baby was missing.

They didn't have much time now. She'd no doubt alert the guards and God knows who else.

There was sudden movement in the hallway. Footsteps. Harried whispers. Then nothing. Jared continued to work on the window, which was no easy feat. Unlike the one in the dining room, this one had double sensor points on each side, which he had to work his way through.

Several seconds passed, before someone touched the doorknob. Just a touch. Followed by another frantic female whisper. Jared heard the baby fret. A sound so quiet that no one would have heard it unless they were listening closely.

Which someone apparently was.

The knob twisted. A fraction. Then, another. The lock held under the gentle pressure, but it wouldn't hold long.

He managed to cut the last wire of the security system and throw open the window. Not wasting any time, he drew his gun and motioned for Rachel to hurry toward him. She did.

But it was too late.

The door suddenly flew open, bits of wood pelting them. Rachel automatically sheltered the baby by turning her back toward the debris. Jared ignored the splinter that slashed across his cheek and tried to shove Rachel behind him.

"I wouldn't do that if I were you," a man called out. Jared saw him out of the corner of his eye. It was Sergeant Colby Meredith. Agnes was right by his side, and she was armed, as well.

"Drop your gun, Dillard," Meredith ordered. "And put your hands in the air so I can see them."

Rachel gasped and buried her face against the baby's blanket, terrified at the sight of the guns aimed at her. Jared could feel her tremble. He hoped she could stave off a panic attack until they were out of there. Now, the real question was—how *were* they going to get out of there?

"Take deep breaths," Jared whispered to her. "And focus. I really need you to focus."

Staring at Meredith, Jared quickly ran through his options. Rachel might have a chance if he could somehow push her out onto the roof while he fired at Meredith. But it was a huge risk—she could easily fall. Neither she nor the baby would survive something like that.

"Drop the gun," Meredith repeated, and he aimed his weapon. Not at Jared. Not even at Rachel. But at the ultimate bargaining tool—the baby.

Jared tossed down his gun immediately. "Play along," he whispered to Rachel. "We'll get out of this. I promise."

This was a plan B kind of moment. Evade and escape. He would have to wait until he was close enough to Meredith and Agnes, and then he'd try to overpower them.

All without getting Rachel or the baby hurt.

Of course, he had to make sure that Meredith didn't kill him first. His fellow officer was probably more than willing to pull the trigger and permanently take Jared out of this equation.

Without taking his attention from them, Meredith reached behind himself and turned on the lights. "Agnes, go put on some tea or something."

That simple order was all it took—the woman quickly scampered out of the room.

However, Meredith obviously wasn't done. He looked at Jared and then Rachel. "Come on. Let's all go back downstairs and have a little talk."

A man in charge. Or maybe that was just what Meredith wanted them to think. Either way, Jared had to wonder if he was finally looking at Esterman's accomplice.

Rachel spoke up. "It's me you want. Let Jared take the baby and leave. You can take me back to San Antonio, and I'll make sure my testimony exonerates your boss."

Jared tried to push her behind him, but she wouldn't let him. She thrust the child into his arms, lifted her hands in the air and started to walk toward Meredith. He also noticed that she closed her eyes. It was probably the only way she could approach the man while he was armed.

The baby whimpered and squirmed against his chest. Jared didn't let it distract him. "Rachel, I don't want you to do this."

Her eyes fluttered open and she glanced at him over her shoulder. And what Jared saw in the depths of those eyes wasn't exactly a look of surrender.

Hell! She was going after Meredith herself.

"Rachel!" he tried again. Jared stooped to lay the baby on the floor. He couldn't let Rachel take on Meredith. It would be suicide.

"You should hold your son a little longer," he

heard someone say. "It might be the last time you have a chance to do that."

Jared's gaze flew to the door. It was Donald Livingston. Smiling.

And armed.

He wasn't alone. There were two other guards with him. Since the infrared had indicated only three adults in the building, these were probably hired guns that had been guarding the bridge. However, it didn't matter where they came from. There were too many of them to fight head-on.

The warden shouldered Meredith aside and strolled into the room. Meredith didn't protest. Sentry-like, he took his position near the door, no doubt to await further orders. Livingston wouldn't have to kill anyone, not when he had Meredith around to do the job.

"Rachel, come and get the baby," Jared insisted.

She did. She must have realized that there was no way she'd get past Livingston, Meredith and the guards. When she finally picked up the baby, Jared eased her behind him. If bullets started flying, he didn't want her in their path.

"How are you this evening, Lieutenant Dillard?" Livingston calmly asked. He motioned toward Jared's weapon on the floor, and Meredith hurried to retrieve it.

Livingston walked closer. Just a few steps. And

from that arrogant swagger, Jared knew he was facing the real boss. Meredith was simply a henchman.

"We figured we'd find either you or Lyle Brewer here," Jared said.

"Brewer? Not likely." Livingston made a dismissive gesture with his hand. "He's a peon, even though he has been invaluable at passing me vital information from Clarence. Of course, Brewer wasn't really aware of that. He's one of those Boy Scouts like you, Dillard."

Jared ignored the comparison. Maybe if Livingston came closer, or if Jared could distract him, he could grab him and use him as a human shield so he and Rachel could get past Meredith.

"So, all of this was your plan?" Jared asked.

"You mean the whole stolen embryo thing? No. Definitely not my idea. Too messy for me. I prefer a simpler approach, but Clarence put all of this into motion before I could stop him. He's a very determined man when he sinks his teeth into something. He got, well, obsessive about getting back at Rachel. When he couldn't find her to have her killed, he figured the baby was the way to do it."

It wasn't an easy thing to hear. His baby and his wife were merely pawns in one very sick game. "Let Rachel and the baby go."

"Touching, but not possible," Livingston said quickly. "I need her alive." He snapped his fingers at Agnes when she came back into the room and motioned for her to take the baby.

Rachel stepped back, but both Meredith and Livingston aimed their guns at the baby. She looked at Jared, fear and worry in her eyes. He nodded for her to hand the child over. This wasn't the time for a fight.

But soon.

Definitely soon.

Agnes walked closer, cautiously, and took the baby. Rachel didn't make a sound, but Jared heard the rough intake of breath and saw her hands clench into fists.

"Don't hurt him," Rachel said softly. "I'll cooperate. I'll do whatever you say."

Livingston placed his hand over his heart. "Definitely touching. But kill him? No. Well, not at this moment, anyway. Later, perhaps. I doubt any of this will surprise you, but you, my dear, are going to go to the courthouse and exonerate my good friend and partner, Clarence Esterman. You will clear him of any and all charges. I want no doubt in the jury's mind that nothing illegal ever went on. And you'll do it convincingly, or else your baby will pay the price. The child might not have been in my original plan, but now I intend to make good use of him."

The warden came closer but stayed just out of

Jared's reach. Jared prayed for him to take one more step, and he might be able to get to him.

"And you, Lieutenant," Livingston continued. "I have a mission for you, as well. After Rachel's finished giving her award-winning performance on the witness stand, and after Clarence walks out of the jail as a free man, you'll be right there to meet him."

Jared shrugged. "Okay, I'll bite. Why would I want to do that?"

Livingston smiled. "So you can kill him, of course."

Chapter Nineteen

Rachel barely heard what Livingston said. She kept her attention on her child. On Agnes. The woman hovered in the doorway, the baby clutched in her arms. Agnes was obviously waiting for her boss to tell her what to do.

"Why would you want me to kill Esterman?" she heard Jared ask.

Only then did Livingston's comment sink in. She glanced at Livingston and saw that he was serious. He really wanted Esterman dead.

"Let's just say that he has the potential to become a liability. He's been chatting with the DA about possibly cutting a deal. I don't approve, and I'd rather not sully my own hands in ridding the world of Clarence Esterman—after your wife has cleared him, naturally. I don't want anyone digging in my direction because of Clarence." He checked his watch. "And without further *ado*, I'll send you two on your way.

When your mission is done, your son will be returned to you. You have my word on that.''

That gave Rachel no hope whatsoever. His word was worthless.

It was as if an iron fist took hold of her heart when Agnes turned to leave the room with Ben. She couldn't lose her baby.

Rachel started after them, but Jared stopped her. "Not now," he whispered.

And just like that, the baby was gone.

Other than choking back some tears, Rachel didn't have time to react. Livingston moved quickly. He gave the nod to two guards, and one of them ordered her and Jared out of the room. They got behind her with those guns so she didn't have to look at them, but it was paltry consolation. No panic attack, but her heart was breaking.

God, what was Livingston going to do with her baby?

They went down the stairs. Quickly, thanks to the guards shoving them in that direction. No sign of Agnes. She'd probably taken their son back to the makeshift nursery. Maybe Livingston wouldn't try to take him off the island.

"What do we do?" Rachel whispered to Jared.

He didn't answer until they were outside and headed toward a boathouse. "On the count of three, drop down. If you can, grab some sand and throw it in their faces. I'll take it from there and try to over-power them.''

Rachel nodded and fought to keep control of her breath. It wasn't much of a plan. A lot of things could easily go wrong. Still, it was a chance, and she'd take it.

''Quit yapping,'' the guard snarled.

Jared ignored him. He did, however, give her a reassuring look when they were only a couple of yards from the boathouse. ''One. Two...''

With the roaring in her head, Rachel didn't even hear Jared say the final number, but she saw the crit-ical word form on his mouth.

Rachel fell to the ground, landing on her knees, and scooped up handfuls of sand. The guard on the left shouted something, and she saw him take aim just as she launched the sand into his face.

He cried out. Dropped the gun. And clutched at his eyes. She didn't stop. Rachel just kept tossing as much sand at him as she could.

Jared used the distraction to go after the other guard. He delivered a judo kick to the man's chest. His rifle went flying, and Jared retrieved it. He turned, and in the blink of an eye, had both men covered.

It had worked. The plan had worked!

''Get in the boathouse,'' he said to the guards. Jared kicked the other man's fallen weapon aside.

Rachel didn't have time to ask Jared what to do next. When the four of them were inside the boathouse, he ordered the guards to get facedown on the narrow deck next to a boat. The boat that was to take them back to shore so the guards could do Livingston's dirty work.

"Move and you're dead," Jared warned them.

And from the tone of his voice, he meant it.

"Rachel, see if you can find some rope so we can tie them up."

She looked around the area, but the best she could do was some fishing twine that she took from a tackle box on the deck. While Jared held the rifle on the men, she trussed their hands to their feet. When she finished, Jared stuffed some rags into their mouths, tested the twine, and then tossed them into the boat.

Then he took her arm and started back toward the house.

They hadn't made it far when she heard the sound. Not gunfire, but something much more frightening.

A helicopter.

And it was about to land on the roof of the house.

"The baby," Rachel managed to say. "Livingston's going to take the baby."

Rachel started to race toward the house but only made it a couple of steps. With her attention on the approaching helicopter, she didn't even hear Meredith step out from a cluster of shrubs.

Jared aimed his gun.

But it was too late.

Meredith latched onto her, hauled her in front of him and put the gun to her head.

JARED'S HEART JUMPED to his throat. The bastard had Rachel. He had her.

Hell, how had this happened?

Jared met her gaze. For only a second. But he couldn't believe the look he saw in her eyes. Not fear. Not even a hint of it. And he knew it cost more to hide the fear than to show it.

"Let her go," Jared bargained. "There's no reason for you to do Livingston's bidding. With your connections, God knows how low you can plea down this case. Turn state's evidence, and you could be a free man."

It was another lie—there would be no plea bargaining for a hired killer—but Jared was willing to do whatever it took to save Rachel.

"I'd rather not call my lawyer right now, if you don't mind."

Meredith's voice was calm. Too calm. Either he was a certifiable lunatic or else he killed as easily as he breathed. Jared didn't want to guess which.

Meredith glanced at the rifle that Jared held. "Put that down. Now." And to emphasize his request, Meredith shoved his gun even harder against Rachel's temple. She winced in pain. ''And, Jared, if there's anyone else waiting in the wings to try to help out, remind them that I can do lots of damage to her before they can even get a shot off. I'm not as committed to keeping Rachel alive as Livingston is. If necessary, I can kill her and Esterman myself, and that way cut out the middle men. By the way, you and Rachel are the middlemen, in case you haven't figured that out already.''

He was right. But not for long. One way or another, Jared would eliminate the threat. Then, he had to make sure Rachel was all right. In the grand scheme of things, Meredith was the disposable one.

''Just go after the baby, Jared,'' Rachel managed to say. ''Save him.''

Meredith tightened the chokehold on her neck. ''Bad advice. Real bad. If you turn to run, I shoot you. It might be quick and relatively painless, but I can promise you, it won't be nearly as nice and neat for Rachel.''

That was enough. It was too big a risk to take. Jared reluctantly placed the rifle on the ground. From the corner of his eye, he saw the helicopter approach. It was definitely going to land on the roof. Once that happened, Livingston could be out of there before they had a chance to stop him.

''Now, step back,'' Meredith ordered. ''I'm going

to take Rachel here for a little drive straight to the courthouse. If all goes well, and if she cooperates, I'll release her unharmed. I'll let you find your own way to take care of Clarence.''

''Why don't you take *me* on that trip instead?'' Jared suggested. ''I make one hell of a hostage.''

Meredith smiled. ''Yeah. I'll bet you would, but I prefer Rachel. She's half your size and a lot less trouble.''

And much easier to hurt.

But Jared didn't get a chance to voice that.

Rachel shouted, the sound of rage and fear. Using one of those Shaolin moves, she rammed her elbow into the man's stomach, pivoted and went after him with her fists. Even though Meredith managed to turn, he wasn't as successful at turning his gun toward her.

Jared caught Rachel and shoved her aside. That didn't deter Meredith. He spun toward Jared.

His gun aimed.

Ready to fire.

Jared had only a split second to react.

He dove for Meredith's feet. Rachel went after him again, as well. Together they knocked Meredith to the ground, and Jared grabbed the gun from his hand.

Jared didn't have time to go back for the fishing line so he could tie up the man. But what now? He didn't want to take Meredith back inside, not where he could continue to be a threat.

With such limited choices, Jared rummaged through Meredith's pocket and found what he was looking for—a pair of thin plastic cuffs. Standard cop issue. But just one pair. Still, it would have to do. Jared clamped one side onto Meredith's wrist, and hauled him to one of the thick shrubs and handcuffed him in place.

When Jared was sure Meredith was sufficiently restrained, he turned to Rachel. "Let's go," he shouted over the noise of the helicopter. "We need to get to the roof."

They sprinted to the house. Jared didn't want them to be out in the open any longer than necessary. Besides, every second counted. If Livingston left with the baby, they might never find him.

Trying to keep watch around them, they hurried up the stairs. Both flights. And came to a narrow door that led to the roof.

The noise from the helicopter stopped. Maybe the pilot had turned off the engine so they could get the baby inside. Or maybe the baby wasn't up there at all.

God knows what he would face on the other side, but since he didn't have a choice, Jared moved Rachel behind him. He took a deep breath and kicked open the door.

He got a glimpse, just a glimpse of Agnes holding the baby. And of Livingston.

Before the bullet slammed into Jared's right shoulder.

RACHEL SCREAMED AND tried to catch Jared so he wouldn't fall.

She wasn't successful.

Livingston was there. Right there. He grabbed her and slung her out of the way. Rachel landed against the wall, and Jared fell just inside the door. So did his gun. Livingston kicked it across the floor.

Rachel came up fighting. For all the good it did her. Livingston merely smiled and aimed the gun at the baby. Both the gun and his murderous expression stopped her in her tracks. She would risk her life without thinking twice, but she couldn't risk the baby's.

"Jared, are you all right?" she asked. She held her breath.

"I'm fine."

But he wasn't. There was a bright red stain making its way across his shirt. She prayed the bullet hadn't hit an artery or a major organ. If so, she didn't stand much of a chance of getting him to the hospital in time. She could lose him. Dear God, she could lose him.

The pilot stepped from the helicopter and aimed

an accusing finger at Livingston. ''You said no one would get hurt—''

Livingston was quick. He turned and fired two shots—both hit the man in the chest. Then he calmly aimed the gun back at the baby.

Rachel glanced at the pilot. If he was still alive, he wouldn't be for long. She wanted to beg Livingston to call an ambulance for Jared and the other man, but it wouldn't do any good. She could see it in his eyes. If Jared died, Livingston would just make other arrangements to deal with his partner.

In his mind, Jared was expendable.

So was the baby.

So Rachel tried a different approach. There was no icy sneer on Agnes's face. She was scared, volleying wide-eyed glances between Livingston and the pilot. Maybe that fear was a weakness Rachel could exploit.

''Agnes, you can't let Livingston get away with this. It isn't right. That's my son you're holding. Do something to stop all of this.''

The woman frantically shook her head and backed up a step. ''I can't. I can't stop anything.''

Jared moved. Just a fraction. Still clutching his shoulder, he leaned closer to Livingston.

Rachel almost called out for him to stop. But she knew in her heart that Jared felt the same way she did. They had to do whatever it took to save their child.

In this case, that meant a distraction, whatever the risk.

"I'll go with you now," Rachel told Livingston.

It was a lie. But it worked. Well, at least it got his attention.

Livingston eased the gun away from the baby. And smiled. The smile quickly faded, however, when Jared grabbed his leg. He managed to knock Livingston off balance, sending the man to the floor.

Jared didn't stop there. Despite his injuries, he dove at him. There was a clash of bodies. Muscle slamming against muscle. Livingston somehow managed to hold onto his weapon and do some other damage. Jared grunted in pain when Livingston landed a punch to his wounded shoulder.

Rachel lurched toward them to help Jared. However, she wasn't fast enough. Livingston threw Jared off him and against the doorjamb.

"No!" Rachel yelled.

Jared groaned in pain but went after the man again. He wouldn't stop. Not until one of them was dead.

Rachel heard a sound and snapped her head toward it. Agnes had kicked Jared's gun her way, and it skittered across the floor and stopped at her feet. The woman had decided to help them, after all.

All Rachel had to do was pick it up.

She sank to her knees and forced her hand to move toward it. But the pitch-black tunnel that her mind created closed around her, narrowing her vision so that all she could see was the gun.

Not Livingston's gun. But the one that had killed her parents.

Livingston shoved Jared aside, slamming him full force into the helicopter. There was no way Jared could get to him in time if Livingston decided to shoot him again.

And Rachel was sure Livingston would do just that.

If she didn't act now, he'd kill Jared.

"You can't do it, can you," Livingston taunted. While he held the gun on Jared, he chuckled. "Clarence told me all about your little problem. Too bad."

She clamped her teeth over her bottom lip to stop it from trembling. Nothing could stop the feeling of terror. Absolute terror. After everything she'd done to keep it away, the nightmare had returned.

And here she was, right in the middle of it.

Focus, she heard Jared say. But he hadn't spoken. Rachel heard the reminder from deep within her heart. *Focus.* Yes, that's exactly what she had to do.

Livingston got up from the floor. Not easily. Obviously the blows from Jared had shaken him. But not enough. He still had his weapon, and, dismissing her, he turned toward Jared.

"Don't you dare shoot him," Rachel warned, her voice a whisper.

Livingston tossed her a carefree smile. "What—do you plan to stop me?"

She nodded.

Just nodded.

Livingston stared at her. A challenge. While he took aim at Jared.

Something slammed through her. Not fear. Nor the turmoil of childhood trauma. Rachel had never felt more in control in her life. She reached down. Her fingers closed around the gun.

She lifted the weapon and turned it on Livingston.

He laughed. And she heard in that laughter what he planned to do—kill Jared.

"You won't stop me," he assured her.

Rachel shook her head. "You are *so* wrong."

Without taking her gaze from his, she aimed low. Curved her finger around the trigger. And squeezed.

The blast was instantaneous. Deafening. The bullet slammed into Livingston's leg. He howled in pain, but even that didn't stop him. He turned the gun toward her.

Just as Jared dove at him.

The men collided and went sprawling. Rachel heard herself scream. They were right at the edge of the roof. The left side of Jared's body was dangling in the air.

"Jared, be careful!" she shouted.

Livingston levered himself up and brought back

his arm so he could fire at Jared. It was a mistake. A huge one. The maneuver off-balanced him. Livingston reached for Jared to try to stop himself from falling.

He dropped the gun.

His hand grasped at the air.

And he plunged over the side.

It took Rachel a second to understand what had happened. Moving back out of harm's way, Jared looked down and shook his head.

"It's over. Livingston's dead."

"Over," she repeated. It was really over.

Still on her knees, Rachel tossed the gun aside and went to Jared as fast as she could.

At the same time, Jared scrambled across the floor. They met halfway, and he hauled her into his arms. "What you did was stupid. God almighty! You never should have gone at Livingston like that. He was armed, and he's a killer. You could have died."

Rachel pulled back and pressed her hand to his mouth. "I'm all right. You hear that? *All right.* You're the one who's hurt. And it wasn't stupid. You would have done the same thing in my place."

She could also tell that Jared wasn't prepared to hear the truth. Maybe later he'd listen to reason. For now, Rachel settled for a quick kiss and helped him to his feet.

"Come on. Let's take the baby and get you to the hospital."

She made eye contact with Agnes and said a quick prayer that the woman would cooperate. Rachel didn't want to fight any more battles right now, but if necessary, she would.

"I'm sorry," Agnes muttered. "I'm sorry for everything."

Agnes's hands were shaking when she walked to them. She held out the baby and put him in the crook of Rachel's arm. Without releasing her grip on Jared, Rachel took her son, pulled him to her and held on tight to both of them.

Chapter Twenty

It was a scene as close to perfect as Jared figured he'd ever see. Rachel and his son napping peacefully on the bed next to him.

He sat up a little, wincing at the tug of the stitches in his shoulder, and just watched them. Unable to resist, he touched his finger to his son's cheek. Ben opened his eyes for a second and then nestled back into his mother's arms.

Jared smiled. Only a new father would consider that tiny event to be a miracle.

The doorbell rang, but he was so happy, it was hard to get riled even by an interruption.

"It's Captain Thornton," Tanner called out a moment later. "Should I let her in?"

Okay. So Jared had been wrong. He could get riled. He'd been out of the hospital only a couple of hours and he didn't want to share his homecoming with anyone, including but not limited to, his ex-boss. In fact, he'd planned on thanking Tanner and sending him on his way as soon as Rachel woke from her much-needed nap.

"This won't take long," he heard Thornton say.

In other words, she was trying to barge her way past Tanner. While it might have been fun to hear Tanner try to stonewall her, this was a meeting he probably should get out of the way.

"Let her in," Jared answered.

As he'd known it would, the sound of his voice woke Rachel. Her eyes were still ripe with sleep when she lifted her head and looked in his direction. The sleep, however, soon cleared, and she smiled at him.

Another miracle.

Jared managed to plant a kiss on her mouth before the captain appeared in the doorway. She stood there a moment and studied them.

"Well, well, Dillard. You've gone all domestic on me. Looks good on you. Both of you," she added, nodding a greeting at Rachel.

"I didn't expect you today," Jared said quickly.

"Yeah. But it couldn't wait."

Dressed in a dull gray pantsuit and wearing her usual sensible shoes, she propped a shoulder against the doorjamb. There were a lot of compliments he could pay the captain. Good cop. Hard worker. Loyal. But fashion sense wasn't something that readily came to mind. And she wouldn't have considered that an insult.

"The chief's pressing me for an update on your condition. I'm supposed to check your boo-boos and give him a report."

Jared eased back the side of his shirt so she could see the bandage. "The boo-boo should be healed in a couple of days."

"Weeks," Rachel corrected. "The doctor said *weeks.*"

She raised herself to a sitting position. As if it were the most natural thing in the world, she leaned over and put the baby in his arms.

"I'll give you and the captain some time alone."

Before Jared could tell her that he didn't want her out of his sight, Rachel brushed a kiss on his cheek and the baby's before she disappeared into the adjoining bathroom.

"Cute kid," Thornton said, walking closer. She peered into the blanket. "I heard the doctor gave him an a-okay. And he doesn't seem to be any worse for wear. He's sleeping like a baby."

"Are you just going to stand there and toss around bad clichés?" Jared asked.

"Nope. Guess it's time to toss something else at you." She sat on the foot of the bed, reached into her pocket and pulled out his badge. She dropped it next to him.

Jared looked at it and then her.

"What?" she barked. "Did you expect me to polish it or something before I gave it back to you?"

"No. But I did expect you to give me some grief about what I did to find my son."

"No grief. Livingston and Esterman put Rachel and you through more than anyone should have had to go through. Still, you owe me. I'm talking about working patrol on New Year's Eve with all those drunks barfing all over your shoes."

He pretended to look very unhappy about that, but it was a small price to pay for what he'd gotten in return. "Thanks."

"Yeah, yeah. What can I say—I'm a sap for a guy holding a cute kid. Brings out all my maternal instincts." She stood and ran her fingers over the baby's toes, which were peeking out of the blanket. "You fed him a bottle and burped him yet? I hear they like to spit up all over the place during that little maneuver."

He tipped his head toward his wounded shoulder. "Hard to do much of anything with this."

"Wuss," she grumbled. But she did it with a wink and a smile. Thornton went to the bathroom door and tapped on it. "By the way, Rachel, you should hear this next part."

Rachel came out. She'd changed her clothes and was wearing one of those thin floaty dresses that went to mid-calf and skimmed along her body. Jared smiled to let her know that he liked her choice of fashion—and that later, he'd enjoy getting her out of it.

"The jury's back on Esterman," Thornton explained. "Thanks to your testimony, Rachel, he's a goner. Life in prison without the possibility of parole. And after browsing through Livingston's computer records, we've managed to round up all their little henchmen. And the final blow—Agnes McCullough will turn state's evidence so she can spill her guts about anything and everything else. That should put a cap on this Esterman-Livingston fiasco."

"And what about Sergeant Meredith?" Rachel asked.

"Ah, the scum sucker. Well, he's behind bars, where he'll stay because Agnes can pin Merkens's murder on him. I hate dirty cops. Hope he gets a cellmate who feels the same way and isn't afraid to show it." Captain Thornton waved goodbye. "Enjoy your new family. You two deserve it," she added before she closed the door.

"We do deserve it," Rachel agreed. She walked closer and glanced down at the badge. "Did you two work out everything?"

Jared nodded. "How do you feel about that?"

"I'm pleased." She lifted the baby from his arms and gently placed him in the bassinet next to the bed.

"I know the danger will always be there. It's part of who you are. I still don't like it, but I'll accept it because I love you. And because I know that badge will never mean more to you than what we have right here."

His response wasn't automatic, not some rote words to accommodate the moment. Jared pulled her to him and looked into her eyes. "You are…everything to me. *Everything.* My hope. My happiness. My future. I love you, Rachel."

The tears came immediately. Smiling, she tried to blink them away. "Just my luck. I wait years to hear you say those words just the way you said them, and I start crying."

"Let's see what we can do about drying these tears."

He ran his fingers over the tiny buttons on the front of her dress. "Considering my injuries, I think sex against the wall is out. Let's try for something equally satisfying but a lot less dangerous. And we might want to do it soon, before Ben wakes up for a bottle."

"But what about Tanner?"

Jared looped his good arm around her and pulled her onto his lap. "He'll have the good sense not to come anywhere near this bedroom with that door shut."

"You're sure?" She smiled. Kissed him. And helped him with the buttons.

"Absolutely. Now, hush and have your way with me."

She did.

HARLEQUIN®
INTRIGUE®

Our unique brand of high-caliber romantic suspense just cannot be contained. And to meet our readers' demands, Harlequin Intrigue is expanding its publishing schedule to include **SIX** breathtaking titles every month!

Check out the new lineup in October!

MORE variety.
MORE pulse-pounding excitement.
MORE of your favorite authors and series.

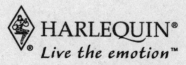

HARLEQUIN®
Live the emotion™

Visit us at www.tryIntrigue.com

HI4T06T

Is your man too good to be true?

Hot, gorgeous AND romantic?
If so, he could be a Harlequin® Blaze™ series cover model!

Our grand-prize winners will receive a trip for two to New York City to shoot the cover of a Blaze novel, and will stay at the luxurious Plaza Hotel.

Plus, they'll receive $500 U.S. spending money!

The runner-up winners will receive $200 U.S. to spend on a romantic dinner for two.

It's easy to enter!

In 100 words or less, tell us what makes your boyfriend or spouse a true romantic and the perfect candidate for the cover of a Blaze novel, and include in your submission two photos of this potential cover model.

All entries must include the written submission of the contest entrant, two photographs of the model candidate and the Official Entry Form and Publicity Release forms completed in full and signed by both the model candidate and the contest entrant. Harlequin, along with the experts at Elite Model Management, will select a winner.

For photo and complete Contest details, please refer to the Official Rules on the next page. All entries will become the property of Harlequin Enterprises Ltd. and are not returnable.

Please visit www.blazecovermodel.com to download a copy of the Official Entry Form and Publicity Release Form or send a request to one of the addresses below.

Please mail your entry to: **Harlequin Blaze Cover Model Search**

In U.S.A.	In Canada
P.O. Box 9069	P.O. Box 637
Buffalo, NY	Fort Erie, ON
14269-9069	L2A 5X3

No purchase necessary. Contest open to Canadian and U.S. residents who are 18 and over. Void where prohibited. Contest closes September 30, 2003.

HBCVRMODEL1

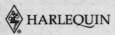
#729 FAMILIAR DOUBLE by Caroline Burnes
Fear Familiar

When Familiar, the famous cat detective, signed on as a stunt double for a movie, he soon found himself up to his whiskers in another mystery! Nicole Paul had been framed and arrested for a theft she didn't commit. After her sexy boss, Jax McClure, bailed her out of jail, the two were swept into discovering who really stole the cursed diamond twenty years ago…*and* the secrets of their hearts.

#730 THE FIRSTBORN by Dani Sinclair
Heartskeep

When Hayley Thomas returned home to claim her inheritance, she found strange things happening around her—doors locked by themselves and objects disappeared before her eyes. The only thing she wasn't confused about was her powerful attraction to blacksmith Bram Myers…but did the brooding stranger have secrets of his own?

#731 RANDALL RENEGADE by Judy Christenberry
Brides for Brothers

Rancher Jim Randall never expected to hear from his college sweetheart again. So when Patience Anderson called him to help find her kidnapped nephew, Jim knew he had to help her…even if it meant facing the woman he'd never stopped loving. This Randall had encountered danger before, but the battle at hand could cost him more than his renegade status.

#732 KEEPING BABY SAFE by Debra Webb
Colby Agency

After Colby Agency investigator Pierce Maxwell and P.I. Olivia Jackson were exposed to a deadly biological weapon that they were sure would kill them, they gave in to their growing passion. But when they miraculously lived, they were left with a mystery to solve…and a little surprise on the way!

#733 UNDER HIS PROTECTION by Amy J. Fetzer
Bachelors at Large

When a wealthy businessman was murdered, detective Nash Couviyon's main suspect was Lisa Winfield, the man's wife and the woman Nash had once loved. Would he be able to put aside past feelings—and growing new ones—to prove Lisa was being framed?

#734 DR. BODYGUARD by Jessica Andersen

Someone wanted Dr. Eugenie "Genius" Watson dead, so her adversary, the very sexy Dr. Nick Wellington, designated himself her protector. But when painful memories of the night she was attacked began to resurface, Genie discovered some shocking clues regarding the culprit…and an undeniable attraction to her very own bodyguard.

Visit us at www.eHarlequin.com

HICNM0903